THE BOMBARDMENT OF ÅBO

CW01335645

OTHER TITLES IN THE SERIES

THE BOMBARDMENT OF ÅBO

A Novella Based on a Historical Event in Modern Times

Carl Spitteler

Translated and with an Introduction by
Marianna D. Birnbaum

Central European University Press

Budapest–Vienna–New York

Originally published in 1889 in German:
Das Bombardement von Åbo: Erzählung nach einem historischen Vorgang der Neuzeit
On the cover:
Russian-Turkish Sea Battle of Sinop on 18th November, Ivan Aivazovsky, 1853

ISBN 978-963-386-573-6 (paperback)
ISBN 978-963-386-574-3 (ebook)
ISSN 1418-0162

Library of Congress Cataloging-in-Publication Data

Names: Spitteler, Carl, 1845-1924, author. | Birnbaum, Marianna D.,
 translator.
Title: The bombardment of Åbo : a novella based on a historical event in
 modern times / Carl Spitteler ; translated and with an introduction by
 Marianna D. Birnbaum.
Other titles: Bombardement von Åbo. English
Description: Budapest ; New York : Central European University Press, 2022.
 | Series: CEU press classics, 1418-0162
Identifiers: LCCN 2022032000 (print) | LCCN 2022032001 (ebook) | ISBN
 9789633865736 (paperback) | ISBN 9789633865743 (pdf)
Subjects: LCSH: Crimean War, 1853-1856--Fiction. |
 Finland--History--1809-1917--Fiction. | BISAC: FICTION / Classics |
 LCGFT: Historical fiction. | Novellas.
Classification: LCC PT2639.P6 B6613 2022 (print) | LCC PT2639.P6 (ebook)
 | DDC 833/.8--dc23/eng/20220707
LC record available at https://lccn.loc.gov/2022032000
LC ebook record available at https://lccn.loc.gov/2022032001

Contents

Introduction

Marianna D. Birnbaum

The novella, *Das Bombardement von Åbo*, is a fun-size treasure, devoted to the Finnish theater of the Crimean war, written by the Nobel laureate Carl Spitteler (1845–1924) of Liestal, Switzerland. The general public knows little about the Crimean War (1853–56) in which the Russian Empire provoked the Ottoman Empire to declare war on October 4, 1853, and Britain and France decided to support the Ottomans.

Best known is the story of Florence Nightingale who with her volunteer nurses worked amid deplorable conditions in the military hospitals of the Crimean Peninsula, and who has been credited with introducing modern nursing. Some might remember the "Charge of the Light Brigade" by Alfred, Lord Tennyson, a romantic poem in which six hundred British horsemen died, as now many historians agree, a meaningless death when heroically attacking a much larger Russian army. Fans of Russian literature may have read Leo Tolstoy's story, the

Sebastopol Sketches about the Battle of Balaclava (October 25, 1854).

A curious fact of that war was that it spread north from the Crimea to the Finnish Gulf. The purpose of the so-called Åland War was to sever Russia's service and northern commercial routes and force her to sue for peace. Indeed, on March 30, 1856, the Crimean War ended with the Treaty of Paris in which Russia formally accepted a humiliating defeat against the alliance of Britain, France, the Ottoman Empire, and Sardinia.

Carl Spitteler studied in Basel where he was a student of the Germanist Wilhelm Wackernagel (1806–1869), whose seminars on the German hexameter and pentameter might have spurred his interest in rhyme and rhythm, and, although just for a short while, also of Jacob Burckhardt (1818–1897), arguably the most famous art historian of his time.

Spitteler continued in Zurich with law and theology and also attended courses in those disciplines in Heidelberg and Basel. He chose, however, neither law nor theology as his profession, but became a tutor in Russia instead, where he worked from 1871 to 1879, paying periodic visits to Finland. His comedic short novel, *The Bombardment of Åbo*, reflects Spitteler's views on the Russia he had experienced.

Having returned to Switzerland, he became active as a journalist and later editor of the *Neue Zürcher Zeitung*. In

1883, he married Marie op der Hoff, an earlier pupil of his. Together with Gottfried Keller and Conrad Ferdinand Meyer, Spitteler was soon regarded the most important figure of German Swiss literature.

Since Spitteler's writing is relatively unknown today and since *The Bombardment of Åbo* is different from his other works for which he was famous and admired at the beginning of the twentieth century, I believe that I should also introduce, albeit briefly, that "other," very different author to the reader.

Carl Spitteler received the Nobel Prize for Literature in 1919, primarily for his *Olympische Frühling (Olympic Spring)*, an epic written in iambic hexameter in which he explored man's relationship to the universe, mixing naturalistic themes with fantastic elements and mythologemes. He worked on what the Olympic Committee considered his *magnum opus* between 1900 and 1905. *Olympische Frühling* somewhat faded during the last century and it no longer speaks to the modern reader. The same is true of many of Spitteler's poems that have not withstood the changes in literary taste either.

Spitteler's essays, especially the political ones and those in which he investigates and analyzes ethical and moral concerns, are interesting to the degree they are informed by the issues of his time, but precisely because of that, have become too meek and obsolete in the face of the much more robust and combative tone of current criticism of the same epoch.

Among his prose fiction, *Conrad der Leutnant* (1898), which had been considered his most "readable" work, having one hero and playing during a twenty-four hour period on a Sunday spent in the pub, still transmits a naturalist vision and structure. *Mädchenfeinde* (*The Young Misogynists*, 1907), the story of two boys and two girls and their short adventure in a forest, next to a river, with the sounds of rushing water and birdcalls, testifies to Spitteler's great talent for depicting his natural surroundings (a decreasing need for those who had begun to investigate the psyche but had no interest in describing a tree). It is a special gift that one discovers and enjoys as it appears in full bloom in his travelogues.

Indeed, the liveliest and most enduring are Spitteler's travel accounts, especially those about the Alps and Italy. It is impressive that even today, when the plethora of films and videos composed about the cultural and culinary escapades of various journalists and celebrities make of the average reader an armchair-traveler, Spitteler's reports and comments have remained so fresh and thrilling.

Before turning to *The Bombardment of Åbo* itself, I think it is useful to comment on Spitteler's most influential piece of prose, the novel, *Imago*, not just because it had brought him international fame, much more so than

Olympische Frühling, but because the novel was a "co-creator" and integral part of the *Zeitgeist*, belonging to that sizable library of contemporary fiction of which much is still read and appreciated.

Imago (1906), Spitteler's only work that has been translated into several languages, tells the story of Viktor, a young poet, who after four years of absence returns to his home town to learn that his "muse," whom he idolized and considered a goddess, had become the wife of someone else. In addition to facing this amorous disappointment, Viktor has to recognize that in reality his beloved is a superficial, middle-class, somewhat neurotic woman whose lifestyle and values he finds intolerable. Nonetheless, in his mind, the elements of Theuda/Pseuda's split persona—the divine muse, the temptress and the disagreeable, bourgeois housewife—share the same soul space. We do recognize the characters with all their variables, including the Madonna and the whore dichotomy, and the goddess and the destructive woman: they are pet topics of the period.

In *Imago*, Spitteler explored the unconscious and therefore played a significant role in the early history of psychoanalysis, although he had little appreciation for the new discipline. Carl Gustav Jung, his compatriot, began investigating Spitteler's concept of "imago," which has subsequently become one of the basic tenets of Jungian psychology: the female image has close connection with the concept of "complex" and "anima" (Jung, 1911). Jung used the term *imago* for the first time in 1912.

Sigmund Freud, who applied the same concept in his work, although less frequently after his split with Jung, named his journal *Imago*, in honor of Spitteler's novel. Remarkably, he co- founded *Imago* with Hanns Sachs (1881–1947) and Otto Rank (1884–1939), in the same year, 1912. In one of the notes to *Traumdeutung* (*Interpretation of Dreams*), he added the following to a later edition, after Chapter IV: "One of our outstanding living poets does not want to hear of psychoanalysis, nonetheless, he discovered on his own the almost identical formula of the essence of the dream: the uninvited appearance of suppressed desires and wishes, masked and pseudonymous."

It is an added, original perspective in which Viktor, the main character, is not merely affected by the three "different" women with whom he is emotionally involved—the *Severe Mistress* (muse), *Imago* (the never attainable female ideal), and *Theuda/Pseuda*, the frivolous wife of a civil servant—but he becomes *the* man, i.e., he leads the life of each man those women believe him to be. He is the cynical dandy, the kindly friend, and the almost insane, love-smitten admirer: Thus, his identity is determined by *the other*. (Here Spitteler's work meets Jung's theory, in which it applies to family relations, and his internalizing an external object is what Lacan later identified as the *Real,* the *Imaginary,* and the *Symbolic.*) "Each" Viktor and each of the women occupy the bodies of different degrees of "value."

As is known, Theuda was a living person, but at some point, as in real life, Viktor's work takes over, and everything else is sacrificed to that. That is the reason why the protagonist, although having suffered many disappointments, may be called Viktor: he triumphs over every obstacle and completes his novel.

Spitteler, who enjoyed giving symbolic names to his characters, even used Tandem (meaning *finally; at long last* in Latin) as a pseudonym for his own early work. Most intriguing is, however, his introduction of *"der arme Konrad"* as one of the characters in *Imago.* As in the paintings of his contemporary, Gustav Klimt (1862–1918), where gold has yellow as its inferior *Doppelgänger,* in *Imago,* too, Spitteler creates a second persona for Viktor: a dichotomy between his intellectual, emotional self and his inferior bodily identity, whom Viktor calls Konrad, his down-to-earth ego, the one prodding Viktor to think of reality. *"Der arme Konrad"* is a well-known 'figure' of German history, going back to the peasant uprising of 1514, first led by Peter Gaiss against Ulrich, Duke of Württemberg (1487–1550). A contemptuous reference to the peasants as *"der arme Konrad"* (meaning *the poor devil*) was revived and—based on *Imago*—became frequently cited in the correspondence between Jung, Freud, and Sándor Ferenczi (1873–1933, founder of the Budapest School of Psychology), referring to their own lowly bodily problems, functions, or ailments.

In another work, an allegoric prose piece, *Prometheus und Epimetheus* (published under the pseudonym Carl Felix Tandem), he exposed the contrast between the two heroes of classical mythology. This work moved Jung to devote an entire chapter to the psychological analysis of the main characters and issues (*Psychologische Typen*, 1921; *Psychological Types*, 1923). Spitteler's later revision (and the use of his own name) as well as the title-change to *Prometheus der Dulder* (*Prometheus the Sufferer*, 1924) might have been influenced by Jung's comments.

Some scholars have mused that Spitteler's negative attitude to psychoanalysis held special attraction for the practitioners of psychiatry, whereas others believed that his interested middle-class readers, who had heard of but never read scholarly works on the subject, enjoyed the "accessibility" of Spitteler's fiction and essays, bringing them closer to the subject. As Hanns Sachs mentioned in his eulogy (1924 [1945]), Spitteler rejected psychiatry because he felt "it would disrupt the work of his instincts." Ferenc Erős (1946–2020) called attention to the "innocence" of his *Imago*.

"Proserpina," a poem of sixteen lines that Spitteler wrote in 1886, seems to be a sketch of *Imago*, a theme that the author later expanded into a full novel. A significant episode appears in both the poem and the novel: a man covers a woman's hand with kisses for which gesture he has no explanation. In fact, also in the novella about Åbo, the reader will notice the moment when the government inspector suddenly does the same; he displays the identical, unexplainable, and instinctive behavior for which Viktor could not find any earlier signals in his mind. Except in *The Bombardment of Åbo*, the dramatic gesture mellows into the comedic.

The "lonely genius," Nietzsche's gift to the period, has not left Spitteler untouched either. He belonged to the late Romantic school of literati, a Nietzschean who believed in the *Übermensch* (superman), the genius who cannot and will not accommodate the trivialities of pedestrian daily life and rather escapes into the world of fantasy. The admiration was mutual: Nietzsche also expressed his appreciation of Spitteler's oeuvre.

The *fin de siècle* is more than rich with works of the same themes: of man and his place in the universe, crises in the modern world, "the *gemütlichkeit*[1] of the inferno," the artist and his surroundings, the impossibility of everlasting, noble love, etc. Clearly, in his fiction Spitteler did not develop new topics: however, he developed

---

[1] Benevolent cordiality.

new approaches (gestural and psychological) to explore the essence of his characters.

The works among which we register his *Imago* are of greater or lesser quality, therefore some did and some did not endure. Spitteler, too, was *Kind seiner Zeit* (a child of his times) and here the stress is on—*not of ours*. The fact that his body of work could not overcome the obstacles of the changing literary fashion—as have Arthur Schnitzler's (1862–1931) or Hugo von Hofmannstahl's (1874–1929), just to mention two of his German speaking contemporaries—might carry a mistaken assessment about its intrinsic values. *Imago* remains a milestone in the literature and thinking of the early twentieth century.

The Bombardment of Åbo, to my mind Spitteler's liveliest and still hugely enjoyable writing, is the least known even to the waning number of admirers of his literary output. The plot, invented for the purpose of exposing the corruption and impotence of many garrison towns in contemporary Russia, centers on an imaginary bombing of Åbo during the Crimean War.

This lightweight comedic piece has many "relatives." It can even be associated with Nikolai Gogol (1809–1853), since in it Spitteler satirizes the political and economic corruption of the Russian Empire (revealed in Gogol's *Dead Souls* and *The Government Inspector*). However, Spitteler's novella lacks the fantastic elements used by Gogol: in his work grotesque motifs are mixed with detailed naturalism, and levity always rules.

The social commentary found in *The Bombardment of Åbo* also follows a long literary tradition in the West and can be compared to the comic, satirical works of Pierre-Augustin Beaumarchais (1732–1799), especially his three Figaro pieces, or the nearly eighty delightful comedies of the Austrian Johann Nestroy (1801–1862). The latter two are closer ideologically to Spitteler: Gogol was a conservative Slavophile, whereas Beaumarchais and Nestroy were liberally minded, especially Nestroy, whose plays are imbued with the spirit of the 1848 revolution. Nonetheless, all three had difficulties circumventing the censorship of their home countries, and so had Spitteler because of his pacifism.

The imaginary plot of the *Bombardment of Åbo* is based on a real fact: the presence of British warships that kept daily life unsure and unsafe in the Finnish and Bothnian Gulfs.

On page one of the novella, the reader is introduced to the brook the Finns call a river, which

"is narrower than a street in a small German town, but it has enviable depth; moreover it quietly meanders across the old capital of Finland. At market time the buyers gather on massive terraces graced by genuine Finnish marble, while the sellers cover the water's entire surface with their boats. The

bridge serves as the Corso on which to stroll, with wooden houses left and right, which despite their shabbiness must not be called modest, because they claim the name of a city. Somewhat further away, but still in the brook, large boats bound for Stockholm are anchored. The sea is filled with an expanse of islets and floating forests; a gigantic lagoon that stretches one third the way to Stockholm. On the opposite side, facing landwards, where the River Aura flows, on a small hill, one can behold the oldest church of Finland which stood there at a time when Stockholm was still a small fishing village."

The waterway that carries the boats, carries the reader into the story.

A nervous mood among the locals provides the backdrop to the novella even before the *"bombardirovka,"* the fictional order for the British man-of-war to bomb the town, actually arrives.

General Baraban Barabanovich Stupenkin, the governor of Åbo (today's Turku), a Russian "on loan" during his country's rule over the region, is entrusted with the town's defense. However, instead of the two regiments promised to him, the general has to make do with one and a half battalions headed by a *"palkovnik"* (a colonel), who constantly disappears to visit the casinos of Helsinki. Thus, Stupinkin has to rely on the man's aide, the limited and lazy Major Balvan Balvanovich, a ladies' man, who excels in card games and horseback riding. He has no other military virtues.

No one organizes Åbo's defense, an increasingly difficult task because the arsenal is empty. Corrupt officers had stolen and sold most of the arms and ammunition. Even the general's horse is gone. In the face of imminent danger, the general addresses the population to animate them:

> *"In a resounding voice, he reminded those present of their duties as subjects, of their good fortune and their prosperity, ever since they had been liberated from the Swedes, and of the fatherly love of the kind Tsar Nikolai Pavlovich who had taken the Finns into his heart with a special love, so much so that once, at the Vyborg parade, he uttered the word "kaksi," with his very own lips."*

Kaksi is the cardinal number "two" in Finnish, but also means "number two" in baby-talk in a number of languages. The fact that the Tsar took the word unto his very own lips turns the entire message into a parody.

> *"The general then continued with a description of the enemy: elucidating their paganism, the outrageous practices of the English, who never honor international law, oaths, or contracts, and depicted for his audience the horrible fate awaiting their wives and children if the enemy left the dark cavities of their*

> *ships and stepped onto the sacred shores of Finland. Finally, he admonished them to resist, down to the knife, called on the young men to volunteer assistance and—now his voice turning softer—declared himself to be ready to accept donations on the altar of the fatherland—namely the drawer of his own writing desk."*

In the classical form of exhortation, General Stupenkin talks to his people, and in those few sentences the reader can learn everything of the governor's character on whose shoulders the fate of the town rests. He is no Henry V.

General Stupenkin and his flirtatious wife, Pelageya Ivanovna are not the true protagonists in the novella. The heroine, the story's central figure, is their clever Russian cook, Agafia, representing the practical wisdom and humor of her class. Agafia's plan to marry her Finnish beau Tullela, and consequently leave the general's service, causes great upheaval in the Stupinkin household. Master and mistress design a variety of tricks to stop her. Their shenanigans fuel this well shaped, delicious comedy of manners, one that would equally enchant us watching it on stage.

There are several serious, in fact existential, issues addressed in this feather-weight, comic presentation of life: social stratification, heartless exploitation, cruelty, and rudeness shown to inferiors. The story reveals a ruling class that accepts no responsibility toward the ruled, where the life of an infantryman or a cook "does not matter much." In the depiction of the meaningless destruction caused by war, Spitteler's pacifism and sympathy for the victims shine through in the otherwise ironically drawn characters and episodes of the story.

Remarkably, of the four protagonists, the men remain weak and passive; the women take into their own hands the arrangements for their future. The reader learns more about Agafia, whose personality becomes a central part of the plot, than about the governor's wife who is mostly signified by her complaining voice. One may think of the pages of *War and Peace* where in the text Russian appears mixed with French. In Tolstoy's Russia the majority who could read, could also read French. In Spitteler's world, there was a need to "explain" Agafia, because his readers knew little about their cooks, but they knew everything about the type the governor's wife represented.

Agafia is a more honest person than her mistress. Both are cunning but one uses her head for survival, the other for money and an easy life, and if needed, for the destruction of others. Agafia pretends to be permissive, free, and easy, but she is not; the governor's wife pretends to be virtuous, but she is calculating and has reprehensible morals. The reader will discover that Spitteler often puts the same sentences in the mouths of two people of different social standing: the identical sentence from the lips of a different speaker, or speech situation, ceases to be the same.

It should be noted that personal names in this story too convey added meanings: *Balvan* may mean idol, but *bolvan* means idiot or blockhead, in several Slavic languages, *Stupenkin* makes reference to the general's questionable intellect, *Tullela* alludes to Finnish pride regarding the musicality of their language, because of its many "l" sounds. Agafia (or Agafya) derived from the Greek word Ogafia (good) was also the name of Agafya Grushetskaya (1663–1681), Tsaritsa of Russia, first wife of Feodor III.

The blue silk dress that Agafia receives from Pelageya Ivanovna, after she had become bored with it, illustrates their relationship. Agafia's learned values are like the dress: hand-me-downs. She believes that if she wears an elegant frock and smokes a cigarette, she will be a lady like the governor's wife who—we know—is no lady. However, Agafia's silk frock has an even more important role: In following its fluffy elegance until the scene where, torn and smudged, the blue gown testifies to the tragedy that has befallen the young couple, we follow the plot that moves the reader from carefree laughter to tears of compassion.

Agafia might be ignorant of history and geography, but she has learned how to navigate in a hostile world. We are rooting for her and are happy that in the end, her naïve belief in God and justice is rewarded, if not by her compatriots, then at least by the enemy. In fact, the final part, in which Tullela receives a generous compensation for his destroyed property, reflects an actual resolution reached in the British Parliament, concerning compensation for damages to civilian property during that war.

In addition to the straight story line, there is an identifiable circle of relationships: everybody's identity gains value by looking down at "the other." The inhabitants of Åbo have domesticated their prejudices: the Russians look down upon the Cossacks, the Swedes, and the Finns; someone is as ingrate as a Tartar, or curses like a Samoyed. When they cannot detest the English whose military superiority is obvious, they call them insane, and ridicule their adversary's belief in "fair play." The Finns, at the bottom of the social ladder, take pride in their local church that stood there when "Stockholm was still a fishing village." And the omniscient narrator, who never enters the story but hovers over the plot, watches it all with a superior wink: he provides a paternal, if not actually patronizing, vision that implies the prestige of hailing from the "civilized West."

Spitteler expressed his deeply held pacifism both in his writings and in his personal appearances. He throws this into sharp relief in *The Bombardment of Åbo*, in which he exposes the irrationality and inhumanity of war. It is noteworthy that he faced attacks as early as 1914, for a speech he gave at the Neue Helvetische Gesellschaft where he spoke about Switzerland, Europe, and neutrality. It was later claimed that his standing during World War I against Prussian militarism and his insistence on Swiss neutrality also contributed to his Nobel Prize.

Although he remains the only Swiss Nobel laureate in literature to date, it cannot be claimed that his is a household name among modern readers, not even in his native country. It might have been because of the general confusion at the end of World War I, or the ensuing influenza epidemic that soon enveloped the world. Whatever the reason, Spitteler's name disappeared from the roster of important writers.

Close to Basel lies Liestal, Spitteler's place of birth. The house in which he was born sports a *Dichter und Stadtmuseum* dedicated to Swiss poets and, mostly, Spitteler. In 2019, several special events were held there, devoted to the 100th anniversary of his Nobel Prize. A seminal volume, *Carl Spitteler: Dichter, Denker, Redner*, published in connection with the commemoration, will, I hope, bring him back to the foreground, because it is painfully clear that the author of a dozen volumes of poetry, fiction, and essays is still waiting for a rediscovery, as does his little *chef d'oeuvre* about the mid-nineteenth century maritime siege of Åbo.

Bibliography

Erős, Ferenc. *Az Imago holdvilága. Carl Splitteler és Szerb Antal* (The moonlight of *Imago*. Carl Spitteler and Antal Szerb). PIM, February 11, 2015.

———. "Szegény Konrád" – Test és imágó az irodalomban és a pszichoanalízisben" (Poor Conrad – body and imago in literature and psychoanalysis). *Imago* 2020, 9(1): 392-404.

———. *Trauma és történelem* (Trauma and history). Budapest: Jószöveg Műhely, 2007, 142–155.

Lacan, Jacques, *Les Complexes familiaux dans la formation de l'individu.* Paris: Navarin, 1984 [1938].

Leuenberger, Stefanie, Matt, Peter, von, [and] Phillipp Theisohn (eds.) *Carl Spitteler. Dichter Denker, Redner. Eine Begegnung mit seinem Werk* (München, Nagel und Kimche, 2019).

Spitteler, Carl, *Literarische Gleichnisse - Vorarbeiten auf losen Blättern, 1890-1891.* II Sibylle, III *Proserpina*, Basel, 1886.02.03

Carl Spitteler

THE BOMBARDMENT OF ÅBO

A Novella Based on a Historical Event in Modern Times

ABO, THE CAPITAL OF RUSSIAN FINLAND.

Everyone knows that rivers can carry large sea-faring ships up-stream, far from their estuary. But anyone who wants to see such giants travel inland in a small brook must make the effort to visit Åbo. Naturally, the afore-mentioned brook does have a name, she is deserving of one, the melodious name of Aura—especially when spoken in a soft southern accent.

The brook is narrower than a street in a small German town, but it has enviable depth; moreover it quietly meanders across the old capital of Finland. At market time the buyers gather on massive terraces graced by genuine Finnish marble, while the sellers cover the water's entire surface with their boats. The bridge serves as the *Corso* on which to stroll, with wooden houses left and right, which despite their shabbiness must not be called modest, because they claim the name of a city. Somewhat further away, but still in the brook, large boats bound for Stockholm are anchored. The sea is filled with an expanse of islets and floating forests; a gigantic lagoon that stretches one third the way to Stockholm. On the opposite side, facing landwards, where the River Aura flows, on a small hill, one can behold the oldest church of Finland which stood there at a time when Stockholm was still a small fishing village.

During the Crimean War, while English warships kept daily life unsure in the Finnish and Bothnian Gulfs, General Baraban Barabanovich Stupenkin, the governor of Åbo, was promised a temporary Russian auxiliary force: two regiments, as it was thought in Petersburg, but in reality they turned into just a battalion and half, headed by a *Palkovnik*[1] who was mostly away in Helsinki and in whose place a Major Balvan Balvanovich acted as their commander. Outstanding in card games and, his obvious laziness notwithstanding, an excellent horseman, except for his proverbial stupidity, the major had no other conspicuous martial qualities. Service, especially after the coast-guard had been organized, led each Russian to permanent, unbearable boredom that, as is well known, had been provided by the Creator for a single purpose: to be chased away with card games.

Here, the unavoidable grand hotel of every Finnish town slowly changed into the *Societätshüss,*[2] the headquarters of the Russian troops which, in addition to the officers, the governor and his wife also patronized. Having served at every imaginable area in Siberia, they still cursed

[1] Colonel in Russian.
[2] Leisure center used as an Officers' Club.

the pitiful nest daily for the past five years, because in Siberia one could at least be sure about one's whist party,
besides the few Russian writers and civil servants whom
one could scrape up in that wilderness. "Not to waste
golden time," as the governor jested in the dining saloon,
they played cards from one o'clock in the afternoon until
late evening, drinking amply, even Swedish punch, at
which the Russians' antipathy toward Swedes and the
English let up for a while, talking politics during shuffling,
namely badmouthing the big and the small powers of
Europe. Even the imperial government of Petersburg
received some needling. During the short pauses or when
she had too few trumps in her hand, the governor's wife
let the young officers court her, and the governor grumbled about how it felt "to be forty-ish."

The soldiers, meanwhile, hung around in the pubs,
drinking and pledging brotherhood with the Finns, or
made a nuisance of themselves at the market, teasing the
female vendors and the Russian peasant women, from
whom, instead of playful responses, they received indignant, moralizing grunts.

That's how things were when one morning, precisely
when the market began to fill up, a Cossack from the
coast-guard, his upper body bent forward, blasted over
the cobbled street.

"*Birigis-jah!*" (Attention!) he shouted as loud as he
could; because the hoofs of his small, reckless little

horse produced only a muffled sound, trailing away in the general chatter.

"What's going on?" a few soldiers asked.

"*Bombardirovka,*"[3] sounded the brief and fleeting answer and the Cossack was already across the bridge.

The word spread mouth to mouth: "*Bumbardirovka*" and "*Bumbardirovanie*" yelled the soldiers to one another and the more intelligent among the Finns who could not translate the endings, but understood "bum," translated it to "*pummi*"[4] and "*tulipummi.*"

In a moment the peaceful market changed into an outraged, indignant, and buzzing mass, looking like a hornet swarm and sounding like a pack of wolves falling upon a horse. The women shrieked, but not as other females would; deep horrible sounds burst forth from them, whereas the men crunched their teeth into one word:

"*Saatanaperkele.*"[5]

Now, hearing the rolling of drums and the sound of horns, the soldiers left.

"God is merciful," they yelled while running in double time. "Finally he sent us something to do."

Governor Baraban Barabanovich appeared on the bridge flanked by four Cossaks on horseback. He was as

---

[3] Order to begin bombing (the ending of the word imitates Russian).

[4] Finnish word for 'bang' (onomatopoetic): the rest is a play on that word.

[5] *Saatana perkele* is a Finnish curse.

elegantly dressed as no one had ever seen him before: in gilded headgear with red and white plumage, a green jacket with heavy golden epaulettes, bedecked by a shop-ful of new medals; over his shoulder, looping down to his sword, a six-inch wide pink band, his pants fire-red, as widely-known, a radiant sign of the general's rank. But he was on foot: he had sold his black horse to major Balvan Balvanovich, which deal, in addition to the de-cent price, had the advantage of enabling him to apply the money that the government annually paid him, for two horses, an orderly, and fodder, for more agreeable purchases. His awe-inspiring view silenced the populace who now listened with cap in hand. The governor spoke. In a resounding voice, he reminded those present of their duties as subjects, of their good fortune and their prosperity, ever since they had been liberated from the Swedes, and of the fatherly love of the kind Tsar Nikolai Pavlovich[6] who had taken the Finns into his heart with a special love, so much so that once, at the Vyborg parade, he uttered the word "*kaksi*,"[7] with his very own lips. The general then continued with a de-scription of the enemy: elucidating their paganism, the outrageous practices of the English, who never honor international law, oaths, or contracts, and depicted for

---

[6] Nicholas I (1796–1855), Emperor of Russia.
[7] The cardinal number "two" in Finnish, but also 'number two' in baby-talk.

his audience the horrible fate awaiting their wives and children if the enemy left the dark cavities of their ships and stepped onto the sacred shores of Finland. Finally, he admonished them to resist, down to the knife, called on the young men to volunteer assistance and—now his voice turning softer—declared himself to be ready to accept donations on the altar of the fatherland—namely the drawer of his own writing desk.

As the speech came to an end, the Cossacks from his own troops shouted *"Urrah"* and a murmur of agreement was heard from the crowd. The governor disappeared and while the troops gathered around the mayor and the pharmacist, the young folk gradually moved to the higher grounds above the town, to procure weapons and get educated in their handling.

As the governor on his way home climbed the steps of his wooden palace, he found the kitchen-door ajar. He immediately muffled his walk, and as if by accident, looked in. Agafia, the delicate, brown-haired cook with her beautiful, almond-shaped *"Little-Russian"*[8] eyes was busy with the hearth. Some distant from her stood a young, flaxen-haired Finn.

---

[8] Malorossiia = Little Russia, which is derived from Malaia Rossiia, was used in official nomenclature in the 18th century to refer only to Left-Bank Ukraine. In 1802 it was divided into Poltava gubernia and Chernihiv gubernia. Ukrainians living outside the Russian Empire were also called 'Little Russians.' Ukrainians did not approve of the term.

"What are you doing here? What's your name?" asked the general.

"Tullela," was the short but modest answer.

"You lazy bum! You should rather defend your fatherland instead of hanging around in the kitchen. Get the hell out here! Godspeed!" Hesitant, the Finn left his place, turning his cap in his hands in embarrassment.

Agafia did not hold her tongue.

"Permit me to tell you, Your Excellency, the fatherland does not matter much, your Excellency! But the Finn is my fiancé."

"You silly goose," hissed the governor. "Are you crazy? You want to marry a Finn?"

Agafia glanced playfully at the fuming man, then confronted him with a cheerful laughter:

"Do you envy him, Your Excellency?" As the governor was ready to burst out in fury, she quickly added, clapping her hands over her knees: "How handsome you are today, Your Excellency! How good you look in this gala uniform!" Then she suddenly flinched: "M'lady is coming," she whispered in a hurry, whereupon the general hastily left the kitchen.

Agafia now took the Finn, who stood there immobile like the holy Alexander Nevsky[9] in the St. Isaac

---

[9] Alexander Nevsky (1221–1263) was prince of Novgorod and then grand prince of Vladimir. A legendary military leader and statesman, he defeated the Swedes at the Neva River.

Cathedral, passionately by his neck, and planted a few kisses on him that the other did not dare to return.

The governor's wife was stretched out on the sofa, smoking. "Have you heard this unpleasant news?" she called out to her husband in her lingering, ever-complaining voice.

"Well, so what? It is still unclear whether the English cannonballs will reach us."

"What about the English? Who cares about the English? The English—they don't matter much! But don't you know that Agafia wants to get married and announced that she will stop working for us?"

"Incredible!"

"Well, have you seen that Finnish bean-pole in the kitchen? You don't have to pretend: I have noticed that you like looking at Agafia. That's natural, she is pretty, and she knows it. But none of this is important now. In any case, I won't let Agafia go. In this pitiful Finnish hole, she is the only one to cook a decent *Batvinia.*[10] What can I do with the best salmon without *Batvinia*? Do me a favor and don't stand so indifferently there: It is your business too."

"My God! Nothing's easier than that. Don't pay off her wages! I hope you have kept some?"

---

[10] Fish soup.

"Don't worry! You can't believe that I would be so stupid to pay her wages in full? She has fourteen months saved with me. However, her beloved is rich: the new, large brick burner up at the beach, behind the town, belongs to him. Can't you take away her passport?

Baraban Barabanovich sighed:

"We don't live in Russia. The Finns are Germans; they don't believe in God and follow no law! This way nothing can be done."

"Then figure out what can be done. It's your business!"

Suddenly a Cossack appeared at the door that, following Russian habit, was always kept open.

"Oh, hell!" yelled the governor noticing him.

"At your service," replied the Cossack politely, and remained standing in the doorway.

"To hell with you, don't you understand me?"

"At your service. But forgive me, Your Excellency, Balvan Balvanovich has sent me. There are no weapons in the barracks."

"That scoundrel has probably sold them! To hell with him!"

"At your service, Your Excellency, but the problem is that we could not find a single bullet."

"Then load the weapons with butter and pickles."

"At your service, Your Excellency, the trouble is that we have just very little gunpowder left."

"What does this have to do with me? This is the business of the Major. Get going! Do you hear me?"

"At your service."

"What a pack of fools!" sighed the general and moved to the window.

At the sight of him the people in the square took off their caps and yelled "*Urrah!*"

"I admit," said the governor's wife in her pleasant, forever lamenting *alto*, "each takes what he can. That's why we have the state and the government. Not for nothing is he major and has a till to manage. But one has to be modest and see to it that there is something left for the others. And, first of all, the fatherland should not suffer. I hope you have written to Petersburg about my cigarettes. You haven't? This is the end! I have only one little box left. For goodness' sake, what should we do here when we no longer have cigarettes?! But to return to Agafia, what do you think?"

Helpless, the general shrugged his shoulders.

"I am calling her right away," she added and clapped.

Agafia promptly appeared at the door. "Have you called M'lady?" she asked politely.

"Yes, to tell you for the last time that I shall never permit you to marry."

"Permit me, M'lady, but it does not matter much what you permit or don't. If you permit, when it is God's wish, I shall marry. Forgive me, but should I prepare the wood grouse[11] with a Swedish sauce as I did last time?"

"Have mercy, you fool! How can you ask such a stupid question? Who would cook game in a Russian sauce! But come here and tell me honestly, do you have any complaints against me? That you definitely want to marry?"

"Have mercy, M'lady! Why would I complain about you? About such a kind, gracious, and nice mistress! Who even gave me a new frock for Easter, and what a beautiful one! I am ashamed to wear it, I look so breathtaking in it. How could I complain about you? I would have to be as ungrateful as a Tartar!"

While speaking, she rushed to the governor's wife and kissed her hand repeatedly.

"Then why do you want to get married? You don't want to tell me that you have fallen in love with that stupid Finn? Such a pretty girl as you! You can get all kinds of husbands! Even the Cossack commander asked you to marry him! And my piano teacher in Helsinki, he, too, is smitten with you! You can count them... isn't that right, Baraban Barabanovich? You are too young to have to rush into a marriage. Wait until my husband is transferred to Petersburg where I will pick a groom for you of whom you can be proud."

---

[11] Wood grouse = capercaillie.

13

Agafia sighed. "I know, M'lady that you mean well, and I am just a simpleminded, silly goose. And my Tullela, I have to admit, is as dumb as a reindeer. Do you think he's capable of putting a single sentence together? Do you think he even once told me how pretty I was, or how nice I looked in my frock? Nothing. Nothing at all! He keeps gaping at me with his mouth wide open, as if I were made of sugar and had red currant brandy in my veins instead of blood. But you see, M'lady, I don't know why: he is so young and totally alone, without parents, without siblings, like a tiny bird that has fallen from its nest. And he loves me, I am telling you, he loves me, he loves me, M'lady, one can't believe how much, like a dog, really, simply like a dog! And therefore, I have to like him too, what can I do?"

"Then go, marry him, what do I care; but this does not have to happen right away. This is no reason to leave my service!"

"Oh, good God! M'lady, you don't know the Finns! They are not as decent as we Orthodox folks are! They are jealous! So jealous that it scares you! And he will not wait any longer. Otherwise, I would not be in this tough spot. But forgive me, M'lady, I have to be back in the kitchen: I left the lox in the skillet!"

"My God! Now you're telling me? And you are standing here babbling, you good-for-nothing girl—Get going! For God's sake! Hurry up!"

Reaching the door, Agafia turned around.

"M'lady, would you permit me to go for a short walk with my Tullela after the meal?

"What got into you? This is no holiday!"

"They're all saying it's going to be a great holiday today; the English are going to carry out a *bumbardirovka*. It should be a lot of fun!"

"Well, I don't care, you can go! Just watch out that no bomb hits you!"

"Thank you," responded Agafia with a friendly bow.

"That would be no great loss either," growled the general ungraciously.

"Thank you," said Agafia, with a giggle, as she now also bowed toward the general. She was ready to rush back to the kitchen, but returned once again, and as if embarrassed, said in a hesitant voice, "Forgive me M'lady, but would you be so kind as to give me a little something from my wages that you are keeping for me?"

The face of the general's wife darkened.

"How much do you need?" she asked sullenly.

"Do you think a ruble would be too much?"

"Nonsense! A whole ruble![12] You have lost your mind! What on earth do you need a ruble for? You don't need that much! Forty kopeks will be more than enough!"

She got up slowly and set about her writing desk reluctantly.

---

[12] Ruble and kopek are Russian monetary units.

"Give that stupid thing the ruble so she can see what's going on with the lox!" shouted the general.

"My God! Good you have reminded me! Off with you to the kitchen!"

The general pressed a ruble into the girl's palm. She kissed his hand twice and also his wife's, then, delighted, she danced out from the drawing room, and seconds later one could hear her singing "The Red Sarafan"[13] in the kitchen.

"What a pity!" murmured the governor.

"I feel sorry for her" said his wife agreeably. "She will go to the dogs. But what is going on with the English? Shouldn't you perhaps look into it?"

"That's all I need! This is the major's business. I am at my post right here!"

One could hear an unusual noise in the square that toned down as the governor tore open the window.

"What's going on?" he shouted in his splendid Herold voice.[14]

"They are bringing an English peace negotiator, Your Excellency," responded a soldier, saluting.

"Tell him, I am busy and let him wait on the street."

"At your service, Your Excellency."

---

[13] Russian song about the red-printed dress worn by girls and women to dances.

[14] Vilhelm Christoffer Herold (born in 1865 in Hasle, Bornholm – died in 1937 in Copenhagen) was a famous operatic tenor.

After a while an officer appeared at the door and reported: "Your Excellency, it is raining."

"That is not my fault."

"I mean that perhaps we should get the peace negotiator under a roof?"

"What for? The English can consider it God's grace that rain is falling on them. It won't harm him. They love water, don't they? What kind of a fellow is he, anyway?"

"He is a marine officer, Your Excellency."

"You see? What did I tell you! Just let him stay where he is." Not much later a second officer appeared.

"Your Excellency, the crowd is growing ever larger and increasingly furious; we are worried that they might do something unpleasant to the negotiator."

"That would not be too bad either. Get out of here!"

The officer was barely gone when the governor regretted his careless words.

"Wait," he yelled after the man. "Take the scoundrel to my reception room. I want to know what he wants from me, although everything is false that these impostors bring up."

A few minutes later, one could hear vague steps on the main floor, and the governor, who after letting the fellow wait for a while, had just decided to proceed in a comfortable speed to receive him, when an armed platoon without an officer, led by a staff sergeant, came marching up the steps.

"What do you want, you dogs?" the general lorded over them. The soldiers greeted him with friendly respect.

"We would like to humbly ask your favor, began the staff sergeant…"

"What favor?"

"To finish him off," he replied persuasively.

"To finish off whom?"

"Just the Englishman," came the response in a cozy tone. A punch in his face smothered the last syllable.

"Does a Russian kill a peace negotiator?" screamed the general, pale with fury. "Are we Tartars, Germans, or Turks? Are we not true Orthodox? Any one of you who attacks or even insults the Englishman will be whipped and shot. Do you hear me?"

"We hear you and we are at your service."

With that they turned around and left; but the staff sergeant stayed, tried to stand straight and expand his chest, while his entire body trembled for fear.

"Your Excellency, forgive me, but I thought to serve God and the Emperor when I wanted to cleanse the world of an Englishman. I was told that they kill small children. And I, too, have children."

"God will punish the English for what they are doing, but a Russian has his faith and kills no unarmed person and no peace negotiator. Understood?"

"I understand and I am at your service. Please forgive me Your Excellency!"

"Go to hell!"

Breathing deeply and thanking his good fortune for the merciful message, the staff sergeant held his hand to his forehead and marched off with shining eyes. The governor left to receive the peace negotiator.

"Can you imagine, Pelageya Ivanovna, what this fellow wants?" he shouted irritably, when he returned half an hour later. "We should pick a house that they would bomb!"

"He is either crazy or is setting a trap for you. How should they recognize the house from that distance?"

"By a red flag that he suggested we string up. I think, he really means it; you know, when it comes to the English, one can believe the most craziest things."

Having made fun of the English for a while, the face of the governor's wife lit up.

"I have an idea: Let them bomb the Lutheran Church. That would be useful as well as a job pleasing God!"

"That's a thought!"

But after a short while, the general returned with the answer: "They don't want to shoot at a church, those hypocrites."

"You know what, my turtledove, let them bomb our palace here. We will get reimbursed by the state, and won't lose a thing! One can accuse the government of a lot of things, but one must admit, they pay generously! And we have ample time to move before the deadline!"

"That's again a good idea!"

Yet, after a while he returned in a fury.

"Now you see what scoundrels they are! They consider it too dangerous: The palace is too close to private houses, and one of the bombs could fly off target!" They suggest we should pick a house that is located outside the center.

"Now, I am having a revelation: Give them Tullela's workshop and the brick burning kiln, then he loses his assets and cannot marry Agafia."

"Our Holy Lady of Kazan[15] gave you the idea!"

He returned after a while, rubbing his hands together. "Good. It will begin at ten in the evening."

The rain stopped during the afternoon and warm sunshine chased away the clouds. Agafia thought to take advantage of her time off and watch the bombardment with her fiancé. Just like the rest of the town's inhabitants, she had no idea of the fact that it would begin only in the evening and that it would affect only the house of her beloved: That remained a state secret, the realm of higher politics. Two dresses hung in her closet, both tempting her eyes. The red one was her national costume that looked very good on her, no question, she heard that often enough, but the other one, the blue

---

[15] *Kazanskaya Bogomater* (Russian).

frock, the gift of her mistress, looked more elegant. The governor's wife had it on at a ball, need one say more? And it had a train—a train! If she went for a walk with the train, Major Balvan Balvanovich would offer his arm and call her "Madame." The train decided it for her and with childish enthusiasm Agafia ran to the kitchen to receive the homage of her beloved. Embarrassed, Tullela removed his cap and took a step back.

"Don't be scared of me!" she whispered graciously while kissing him, "for you, I shall always remain your little Agafia."

They moved out onto the street, arm in arm, and Agafia, who used her parasol back and forth as if it were a fan, enjoyed with satisfaction the sensation she had generated. he Finns gave way in respect and reverence, the soldiers saluted, and even the officers and the civil servants, having stared mockingly at her companion, offered her more or less voluntary greetings. The train has done its duty. Now, Agafia lacked but one item to be distinguished: cigarettes. However, she had a ruble and there was a pub nearby. Leaving her beloved standing, swiftly, like a squirrel, she rushed up the steps of the inn and bought a package of "La Ferme."[16] She reap-

---

[16] La Ferme Company, which won a prize at the Exposition Universelle de Paris in 1879, was one of the major tobacco producers in Russia. The Tobacco Factory "Laferme" ("Society of Tobacco Products") was founded in St. Petersburg in 1864.

peared wrapped in a cloud of smoke, coughing loudly, with the cigarette between two of her fingers held far away from her body.

She finished one off every half a minute, and would then ask the next passer-by, preferably a civil servant, for a light. The men bowed politely and gallantly, touched their hats, and provided what she requested.

Instinctively, the couple chose the road leading to the port. There they found everything in the wildest commotion, because the English warship had just arrived between the islets and anchored menacingly in the nearby distance. One could actually distinguish the two rows of cannons and the bulging sails that towered over the pine trees on the islands.

"How lovely! What a festive day!" Agafia cried out, clapping her hands in delight.

This aesthetic judgment was disapproved by the people around and they responded with wild threats.

"Do me the favor my friends, and don't be scared!" Agafia appeased them, "the English do have cannons, but whether they have gunpowder or cannonballs that is a different question! Believe me, it will be with them as it is with the others. In the beginning, when they leave home, they have everything; but England is far away and life on the ship is boring. Today the admiral sells a small cannonball, tomorrow the captain sells another one for a lady's hat, or for a corset, or a pair of little lace-up boots;

the sailors exchange gunpowder for snuff and cigarettes—after all, what else could they do with gunpowder? And they also need brandy, the poor fellows, even
if they are English and not true believing Orthodox!
You see, they just sell a handful of gunpowder each day,
but by the end of the year—you understand?—when it
comes to shooting to kill, how much gunpowder and
cannonballs have those poor souls left? Nothing! Simply nothing, I am telling you!"

The Finns started to see the light, and began to mum-
ble comfortably. Yet, some choleric types were unable to
tolerate the view of the monster that came to bomb Åbo.
They climbed onto a small coastal steamer and amidst the
wild cheers of their compatriots, set out for an attack at
sea. On the English side, first signs, flags, and pennants
appeared; suddenly a strong red light burst forth from the
broadside of the ship, wrapped in a brown-blue cloud,
followed by a soft but powerful thunder.

"Pummi" screamed the Finns on the riverbank, and
howling with rage they tumbled over one another. Since
nothing more happened, they gradually pulled themselves together and asked about the number of dead.
No one was even wounded, nor was any cannonball either heard or seen.

"What did I tell you?" yelled Agafia triumphantly.
"Now you see that I was right. They don't have cannonballs."

A mounted courier arrived with the speed of a whirlwind and relaying strict orders, he brought any cravings for further attacks on the ship to an end.

"Come, my turtledove, there will be nothing more here. Let's go along the coast to the Cossacks. There is always some celebration there. With the Cossacks every day is a holiday."

On their way, on Henrik street, which imperceptibly wend its way through the rural landscape like a village, Agafia misbehaved at every turn. Like a weasel, she pushed her tiny nose into open windows, and teased the old, while giving affectionate hugs to the children. Soon, she straightened her back like a peacock, and sweeping the street with her delicate blue evening gown, cast a fiery sideways glance at male passers-by, something she took careful note of while watching the French divas in the *Societätshüss*. Imitating them, she believed herself participating in the life-style of the finest of the fine, even in Petersburg. Tullela, who had no idea what was taking place, walked respectfully by her side, and let it all happen.

Outside the town, in a meadow, they spied Major Balvan Balvanovich, inspecting the infantry. Suddenly startled from his card playing and knocked for a blow by a note from the governor threatening him with a court-martial for the theft of weapons, the poor man totally lost his head. To retrieve it, he galloped in circles around the small troop, insulting the soldiers and reproaching the officers in a polite yet whining tone, while letting forth terrible blasphemies left and right that make even a Samoyed blush. During this abrupt fit of fury, the officers went on smoking indifferently, whereas the soldiers stood impeccably at attention, and those who had no weapons, carried out their exercises according to regulations, sporting their imaginary rifles alongside their armed neighbors. From time to time, Balvan Balvanovich would lose his breath; then he would ride up to the small mound upon which Mademoiselles Titi and Fifi, the stars of the *Societätshüss*, were enthroned, honoring the inspection with their presence. Taking a deep breath in front of them, he dried the sweat off his forehead with his handkerchief and complained bitterly about a fate that had condemned him to take orders from "such a barbarian, brutal Russian gang," instead of, as his talents had predestined him, to be born a field-marshal in the army of Napoleon III for whom he developed a passionate enthusiasm that day. After he had invited the ladies to genuine Vyborg Cognac, he opened his collar, baring his skin, kicked his horse on both sides with his spurs, and returned to dressing down the troops.

Agafia, proud and aware of the elegance of her silk frock, and pulling her fiancé with her, walked slowly along the front line of the troops. She led a private parade. Having completed the inspection and found everything to her liking, she planted herself next to Fifi and Titi, and made it her business to outshine the Parisian women from Brabant, turning them yellow in fury. No position was too theatrical and no contortion too graceful for her to try. Since she was a beautiful young creature, even with the greatest desire and most honest effort, it was absolutely impossible for her to appear to her disadvantage. She therefore immediately achieved her intention vis-à-vis the worn-out second-rate singers. This led to a mixture of gloating and shoulder shrugging, like when three female turkeys fight over a male. Since neither party understood what the other was saying, it did not lead to peace when each was listening to the squawking of the other, telling everything that was on her mind, because it reached her opposition merely as a pantomime.

"You see," laughed Agafia delighted, gesturing animatedly, "what irritates you is nothing but envy. That I am now a fine lady, that I smoke *La Ferme*, because I have a fiancé, a young, handsome and rich fellow who does what I want, who carries my sheepskin coat for me, who buys me raisins on Sunday, a whole bag, and each day carries up the firewood for me for the kitchen. That's what you would want, too. Isn't it? But, your efforts here are in vain for he is faithful to me and loves me. He loves me, I am telling you, like a baron, he loves me as if we have been married for fifty years and have grandchildren together; he loves me like 'Elija the Thunderer'[17] even if he does not believe in the true church."

At this very moment, displaying an uncertain reverence, Balvan Balvanovich rode up to them, attracted by Agafia's flounce dress, shining from far away. Agafia made a deep and coquettish bow, followed by a mischievous squint, and chattered with comradely intimacy: "Do you remember me, Balvan Balvanovich? How do you like my looks? Why so furious? Today is a holiday! You must not take it to heart when Baraban Barabanovich says something unfriendly to you. He does not mean it; I know him well. Deep down he is all heart even if he speaks too harshly at times. He comes to see me in the kitchen every day and chats and plays with me for hours like a child, not the least stuck up, he holds my neck and kisses me like a simple soldier, sits at the hearth like a German cockroach,[18] and is not offended when I pour water on him. And he sings, I am telling you, he can sing, you won't believe it, just like a Cossack. He has one fault only: he is a touch jealous. But one should not blame him for this. He is the master of the land."

Indeed, the major's features softened and his glance became friendlier as he followed the graceful and flirta-

---

[17] The prophet Elija is also called Elija the Thunderer in the Russian Church. His name is celebrated on July 20.

[18] *Blattella germanica*, the most common cockroach.

tious movements of the girl. However, when he offered her a bottle of corn schnapps, and showed his intention to get off his horse, she refused him in the affected tone of a very busy person.

"Forgive me, Balvan Balvanovich, I have no time; I have to introduce my fiancé to the Cossaks; they don't know him yet. And they have music, most probably there will be dancing. As for the Englishmen, don't fear them in the least. They haven't any cannonballs, I know. And on land—everyone says so, ask who you want—they don't know how to move at all. God took their legs away."

Then she curtsied and wiggled as she left, but not before she waved a cheerful good-bye to the troops with her handkerchief, happy with her victory over Fifi and Titi.

Noticing that Tullela had turned beet red with jealousy, she began to admonish him gently but firmly:

"Look, Tullela, my turtledove, forgive me, but you are dumb as a reindeer. One cannot hold it against you that you are not a true Orthodox and therefore you don't know how to behave. First of all, when one accompanies a lady, one does not slouch behind her, but puts one's hand on her arm.—This way! Then one goes together, as one person, with toes pointing nicely outward.—Just like that!—And one does not look at the ground, but around, making sure others have seen him too. Then one says to me 'Mignon' in French: that is elegant. Say 'Mignon'! Good; not bad at all! You are not as clumsy as you look, one just has to educate you a bit. And, you know," she whispered more tenderly, "when we are married, I will be your good and loving wife, and will never fight you. We will sit all day on the swing, arm in arm, and smoke cigarettes, and in the evening we'll let the Cossacks come and they will play the accordion for us. And each Sunday I shall buy candles from the priest that he should pray for you not to end up in hell."

Gradually, in the absence of others, and encouraged by the familiar landscape Tullela's became more at ease. He became monosyllabic, later even chatty, called her by all kinds of nicknames, now "salmon," now "butterball," and described how he had furnished for her his new house at the brick factory, with brand new furniture, that she should not lack in anything, there would be beautiful wide beds, and a large, light kitchen.

In making this description, his eyes shone and, animated by the memory of his labors, he illustrated his words with awkward movements of his arms. Greatly pleased, Agafia smiled, nodding from time to time. Suddenly she stopped.

"But sugar," she asked with some eagerness, "I hope you have not forgotten sugar for the tea? We are rich, after all. We can fill up the entire cup to the rim, and don't need to hold the little cubes between our teeth and sip the tea through it like the peasants and the merchants. And if God gives us children, the boys will have to study Baron like the Germans, and the girls will be great ladies, so that when the emperor visits Finland and asks, "What kind of people are those?" I shall respond, "They are my people, Your Majesty, they are mine!"

Amidst such conversation they reached the first guard of the Cossacks.

"What are you doing here, you lazy-bones?" asked Agafia of the longhaired lad, who lay stretched out on the ground next to his horse, "why are you not at the dance?"

"There is no dancing today," responded the fellow sourly. "Today, there are the English."

"The English don't matter; what do I care about the English? I am rich. I have a ruble on me, I'm buying! Where are your brothers?"

The Cossack pointed in the air toward a headland, then turned away from them without pulling in his legs.

Agafia's dress caused such amazement and respectful admiration in the Cossack camp that even her trusted dancing partners and brandy-brothers scrambled up from the ground to greet her with a formal bow. Agafia accepted graciously, although as she fluttered by them daintily, she chirped cheerful little nonsenses to some of them.

"What are you doing here, brothers?" she took up with them, and without any further ado, she sat down on the wet grass, half disappearing in her flounced dress and train, like a hen in her nest.

"What are we doing, Agafia? What are we doing? Well, what will we be doing?! Well, I think, we will be doing as always. It is God's will. In the morning—we'll do nothing and in the afternoon… I have no idea. What else can we do? But, you, what news do you bring?"

"What news do I bring? Me? What do you want me to bring? I bring good news. I bring a holiday. So there!"

With that she searched in her pocket and let a copper-piece fall to the ground. The Cossacks threw themselves upon it excitedly und fought over the coin. Enjoying the performance, Agafia nodded approvingly and with a festive look on her face, she searched her pocket for a second time, then a third, and then a fourth time, and so on, until she was down to the last kopek. In a few seconds, three bottles of brandy and two old and dusty glasses appeared, shimmering with iris-colored hues. Agafia motioned her fiancé to sit down beside her.

"Permit me, brothers" she spoke with great seriousness, "that I introduce my fiancé: a decent, faithful, and rich man, and you might or might not laugh, it is I as true as I am sitting here, he never gets drunk, not on Sundays, not even at Easter, he is so fine and distinguished."

The Cossacks looked respectfully at the man who never got drunk, while his awkward Finnish style provoked their need for mockery.

"Don't bother him, I am warning you," Agafia added in earnest, "even if he is just a Finn, because he loves me, and he is mine."

With an amorous look on her face, she flirtatiously poured a glass of brandy and handed it to Tullela. The rest she poured in a glass for herself and draining it with a loud gurgling sound, she snapped her fingers to refill the glass, and, looking important, she handed it to the Cossack standing next to her.

"To your health, brother!"

The fellow bowed so deep that a strand of hair fell over his face and he responded with laborious courtesy: "To your health Agafia. Forgive me that I am so forward."

And that's how it went down the entire line.

"What is this?" grumbled an enraged voice into the heap of drunks. The Cossack headman looked at the boozers with an angry face.

"Well, what is 'what'? Your Honor!" rang out in a chorus of flattering and pleading tones, "what is this 'what' going to be? A little holiday." And two glasses were lifted in hospitality toward his lips. Meanwhile, with a patronizing gesture, Agafia offered him to sit down in the grass.

"Don't be embarrassed, Your Honor! There is plenty of room here! Unless," she added with a sassy glance, "you find my closeness unpleasant."

The headman could not resist the French ball-gown; his features became softer and his merry Cossack eyes began to throw brazen glances around. Finally, frank and free, he took a seat next to the pretty Agafia, while his decision was honored by a reverent but thundering applause.

As if longing for him, Agafia poured him a glass, put a cigarette in her own mouth and pressed another between the headman's lips with a smile that would have sufficed to fire up each and every Cossack from the Don River to the Caucasus. Thereafter she slipped an arm around his waist and whispered:

"Would Your Honor like to dance a little?"

The headman shook his head sullenly, and spit out his cigarette. "No" he said briskly. "Today, it is forbidden."

"But why?"

"Because."

"Oh, I know why dancing is not permitted!" cried out Agafia indignantly, moving away from the headman. "I know. For no other reason than the English. I understand. I understand. You are scared of them, Your Honor, just like a little speck, quite like Balvan Balvanovich! Have mercy on me! Do me a favor! To be scared of the English? Ha-ha-ha! A great reputation, the

English have! So, you also believe in the *bumbardirovka*, here in this camp. Permit me, brothers, but I find you ridiculous. *Bumbardirovka!* You just don't know. But I do! And I am going to tell you. I, Agafia, will tell you!"

With these introductory words she placed herself in a flattering position and delivered a well-articulated speech in a loud voice convinced and certain of victory.

"You see, brothers, things are like this: You know the Crimea, down there, far, far, far away? And still further away than the Crimea and the sea, and even further than the Caucasian Sea, and still further away than the Caucasus, is Yevropa[19]: Tartars and Turks, and Constantinople and Paris and Stockholm and all that. And Napun Leonovich,[20] the German tsar in Paris? And Yevgenia Napunleonovna,[21] his wife, think about that!"

"Europi is there!" interrupted Tullela, correcting her with a growl, pointing his arm toward the West.

"Be silent, turtledove!" ordered Agafia tenderly but firmly. "Be silent, listen, and learn! As I was saying, brothers, you see that Yevropa is evil and does not believe in God, and does not want that Christians should go on living; that's why she helps the Turks. But because Russia is an island…"

---

[19] The words "Jevropa" and "Europi" ridicule Agafia's uneducated Russian and Tullela's Finnish pronunciation of the word Europe.

[20] Napoleon III (1808–1873), French emperor.

[21] Eugénie de Montijo (1826–1920), wife of Napoleon III. Empress consort of France.

"Russia is not an island," muttered Tullela, irritated.

"If you won't hold your tongue, my treasure, people will tell you to go away. You were told to be silent, do you get it?"

"Keep silent!" affirmed the choir menacingly.

"Brothers, have mercy! It is not an island!" he said. "Why isn't it an island? How so? You have eyes, Tullela, you too have eyes! What is it then? Between the islets— what is that? I believe it is the sea. What else? In any case, no soup and no ink! And the boat of the English, what do you think Tullela, has arrived by the train that runs between Moscow and Petersburg, or on a three-wheel telega?[22] And Helsingfors[23] also has the sea, I saw it myself, and Vyborg too, and in Archangelsk, as I heard, there is the sea again, and in Novaya Zemlya— the sea, everyone says so, and at Astrakhan and at Kamchatka, everywhere, everywhere! And that is why the Germans in Yevropa have to build ships, the poor things, if they want to attack Russia, big, big, ships and many, many of them! But that won't help them at all, not a mouthful, not a tiny glass of schnapps, not even a drop, because God and the tsar are friends. And God is cunning, but you have no idea of that. How should I

---

[22] Telega, a horse-drawn cart used by Russian peasants.

[23] Helsingfors, the Swedish name for Helsinki and the primary name of the city when part of the Russian Empire. Pronounced Gelsingfors in Russian.

make it clear to you? Well, I have it! Brothers, do you see, do you understand? Think of the Tartars: Isn't a Tartar capable of outsmarting three Cossacks? And one Cossack outsmarts six Russians, and one Russian twelve Germans and Englishmen. But a single angel is shrewder than a hundred Tartars, even the slyest. There are millions of angels, many, many millions, more than mosquitos, money, or crows. And the angels also have their *palkovniki*, who swindle them, and the *palkovniki* have their own ministers, who cheat them, and still God alone has the right to have them deceive one another. Do you understand it now? Do you get that finally? The Germans and the Yevropeans must die fighting one another, the poor souls, because they are helping the impious!"

"But there, in Crimea, we heard, things don't go well," a Cossack tried to interject.

"They go bad," grunted the headman.

Agafia laughed heartily and clapped her hands together.

"How stupid you actually are, brothers! Forgive me, but let me tell you, and don't get angry: Don't you understand anything? It is crystal clear that God set a trap for them. I told you he is cunning. Just watch how he thinks things through. First he draws them all into Sebastopol, more and more of them, until no one is left at home but women and children. Then, when he has them all together, he closes the hatch. Bang! Trapped!—You know what I think?" she whispered, while stealing a sidelong glance at the sea. "That warship you see there, that is the last one: God allowed them to escape from the trap. And in their fear of the Russians, they ran away from the Crimea with the ship, just running without a stop, all around Russia, running, running, without rest, day and night, until Åbo. That's that. Brothers, give me some brandy, please!—If it is permitted."

A murmur of agreement honored the political education. The headman, seduced by the charming and melodious chatter, wanted to sling his arm into Agafia's.

"No, Your Honor," Agafia resisted whispering, but knitted her brows in earnest. "This is forbidden. You must learn that my fiancé does not believe in God: he is jealous. It's true, he does not say anything, but before you know it, he has the knife in his hand. Really! So help me God! How about taking a little walk, Your Honor?"

She got up solemnly, let the silk gown rustle about her, drew herself up, tilted her neck to the side like a lovesick swan, moved her outstretched arms back and forth, and wriggled toward the sea, staring at everything that lay before her eyes: the sparse daisies in the grass, the shimmering pebbles on the shore, the enemy ship close to the archipelago, because it was a holiday. In between, with overwhelming tenderness, she caressed the scruffy little Cossack horses.

"But you know what, brothers?" she cried and looked around suddenly amused. "Let's play a little bit with the English. Take the horses down to the beach, and put them with their backsides to the English to aggravate them!"

Always ready for a practical joke, the Cossacks immediately set the idea into motion, and with sweet words and friendly clicking of their tongues, led the clever little horses down to the coast, lined them up with their heads pointing inland, and by pinching their ears, made them kick their hind legs high in the air.

"Good, boys! That was well done, brothers!" Agafia praised them earnestly. "Heroes, simply heroes. No more, no less."

The headman, who for a while did not let Agafia out of his sight, now crept closer, touched her with an intimate elbow nudge, and whispered:

"How about dancing, huh? How about it, Agafia?"

Impertinently, Agafia made a mouth.

"No, thank you!"

"But why not?"

"I don't want to. I am tired."

"Nonsense" shouted the Cossacks. "Hurry up, Agafia, come and let's dance!"

Contemptuous like a baroness and bored like a queen, Agafia showed her back to them. Meanwhile, the Cossacks, not bothered one bit by her refusal, formed a circle and got hold of an accordion.

Forgotten and rejected by everyone, Tullela stood apart, looking gloomily at the ground. Agafia, nimble as a deer, pranced up to him.

"Don't be angry, my turtledove! Don't be sad, my darling! Having a little fun should not make one sad. A little dancing, nothing more. Anyway, I love only you. And then we'll get married. Do you want to? But get in the first row so you can admire how I dance. And keep your eyes open, there will be something to see."

After she gave him a few swift and furtive kisses, she dragged him to where the soldiers were standing.

The accordion squeaked out a minor chord. As the festivities required, the Cossacks stared with a vacant look at their boots; then with blaring cries, they burst into one of the unpronounceable and unending laments in *presto furioso* that down along the Dnieper River serve the population as the symbol of rejoicing. The headman, who pulled the black butter pail brazenly over his left ear, chewing the leather strap flirtatiously with his teeth, asked for Agatha's arm in French, and strutted around with her in the center of the circle. Then he released her with a bow from the times of Louis XIV, and proceeded to show her his best skills, twirling about her as if possessed, first squatting on the ground and tossing his booted legs about ever faster like the devil out of a box; soon he did the Cancan, then, with his sable in his right hand, he fought some attackers as if he were ready to jump over ramparts or conquer trenches. During this labor, rivers of sweat ran down his forehead and long strands of hair remained matted to his face. Agafia, meanwhile, turned and twisted like a snake, fluttered her handkerchief in the air, trying to attain the gracefulness of an elegant lady, honest and respectable. She cast self-satisfied glances up and down, left and right, until the crazy speed of the endless and blasting song finally won over her affectedness, upon which like a Kobold, she danced the Cancan with bold steps in her kitchen boots, while the whirling and twirling of her muslin frock took the singers' breath away. Whenever she passed Tullela, she gave him a penetrating, loving look.

Tullela, who in fact was very proud of the artfulness and success of his fiancée, glanced suspiciously from one Cossack to the other, and from time to time, murmured to himself, "She is mine."

In the evening, around ten, still in broad daylight, the man-of-war traveled under full sail among the islets of the archipelago and anchored within shooting range. This sight caused an immediate and tremendous excitement among the burghers who remained unaware of the agreement between the governor and the English. The street swarmed with people like an anthill; men of military age, armed with knives, fishhooks, and threshing flails rushed down to the port, or north and south of the town, toward the beach, letting out wild curses, ready to fight; the more frightened part of the population hid in cellars or in the churches; some courageous women began collecting water in kettles, pails, and buckets expecting fire damage, because Åbo did not sport a fire brigade at that time. Delegations of Finns and Swedes took turns offering suggestions to the governor what measures to take; the two Lutheran pastors, however, and the mayor brought up the value of the irreplaceable thirty thousand human lives about whom one would have to give account at the Last Judgment, and begged that the town be given up, all the while expressing with enthusiasm their everlasting attachment to the emperor. For all these irrational demands, the governor prepared the same response: "Good, my friends! Excellent! The Fatherland thanks you. By the way: this is my responsibility. Therefore, please do not worry about this any further." As the pastors and the mayor grimaced and brought up the issue of nursing mothers and minors, he suddenly lost his patience.

"My palace is not an institution for midwives. If you are keen on children's shows, as far as I am concerned, you can perform the comedy in the *Societätshüss* or in the church, or wherever you please. Now, enough of that! You can all do me a favor! It has been a pleasure, Gentlemen."

He ordered the troops divided and had the compa-
nies separated widely from one another, mostly south of
the town, inland, in the vicinity of the palace, as far away
from the kiln as possible, that they should not be in the
way, but ordered one battery of four cannons close to
the brick factory, just for show. He and his wife, ac-
companied by Balvan Balvanovich, the general staff, and
half a company of Finnish guardsmen, set off in the di-
rection of the target of the *bombardirovka*, toward a small
hill north of the town, close-by Tullela's house and shed,
straight above the sea, where the *Hôtel de l'Océan* pres-
ently stands with its painted marble pillars made of
larch-wood,[24] showing off their faux shine. They took
up positions at the bottom of the hill, in a hollow nook,
where one was more or less removed and protected, but
could still observe the ship as well as the flag that the
governor ordered to be placed on the top of the kiln so
that the enemy should not miss the target.

Balvan Balvanovich, plagued by his visions of a court
martial, crouched on his tall, black horse with an empty
stare; the helmet seemed to have made his low forehead
even narrower. All his attempts to involve the governor
in a comradely conversation drew only contemptuous
glances and disparaging remarks. Now he approached
the governor's wife, scraping together and applying with
the greatest effort his clumsy gallantry practiced up to

---

[24] Siberian larch is a softwood tree native to western Russia.

then only on women performing in cafés or working in bathhouses.

"I beg you," he raised the issue, "Pelageya Ivanovna, you are exposed here to the cannonballs. Would you not want me to accompany you into town? I shall order a company for your protection."

"No, thank you," came the ungracious answer, "I love cannonballs."

"In that case, I am at your service. May I accompany you up to the top of the hill?"

"No, it is drafty on the top."

"It's drafty? I hope, you are not unwell, Pelageya Ivanovna?"

"Good God! What a meddlesome person! I have a pain in my chest."

"On which side, if I may ask? On the left side or on the right?"

"*Durak*,"[25] hissed the governor furiously.

But he did not give up.

"Your delicate, velvety legs, Pelageya Ivanonvna, will get tired standing here for so long. May I offer you my horse?"

The general's wife looked at the beautiful, fiery animal with instinctive pleasure. Accommodating, Balvan Balvanovich jumped off and urged her to mount the horse.

---

[25] Durak, a Russian word for blockhead or fool.

"Please," he spoke politely, holding the stirrup.

Pelageya Ivanovna took a look at her frock (not a riding outfit), another look at the troops and hesitated.

Balvan Balvanovich knew what she was thinking.

"Officers—withdraw!" he commanded urgently.

Feeling reassured that the command would be followed, she raised her body adroitly in the saddle in the male fashion, and her enervated posture suddenly transformed into one of the bold, amazonian Graces. Her eyes lit up. Happy under the light weight and the soft but secure handling of the reins, the horse began to prance, snort, and whip its tail.

"Fine." The governor's wife thanked the major, nodding graciously.

The fellow breathed a sigh of relief, still panting and puffing over the fear that just vanished.

"You see! Thank God! Now everything will be much better!" he mumbled reassuringly. "A general's wife, young, soft, and neat is the best means against a court-martial."

The frigate shot a projectile in the air, followed by a second and a third.

"This means, it is beginning," mumbled the major phlegmatically.

From the first ship's hatch, on the left-hand side of the highest row, a little blue cloud undulated, rustling and hissing, and spat something into the birch bush down below at the brook, behind the brick kiln, shredding the branches. A thunderous shot cracked from the distance.

"Missed!" remarked a gunner, calmly. And the rest of them repeated nonchalantly: "Missed!"

From the next hatch, a second cloud of smoke followed the first. A cannonball came dancing along the sea's surface, bouncing merrily up and down, spraying about water and foam. The soldiers were roused.

"Watch it, brothers!" spoke an officer, thoughtfully and seriously. "Now it's happening in earnest."

In any case, the third grenade exploded in front of the house, hurling around turf and clay on its way down to the hollow nook, where it spread dust and dirt on those standing there. A happy laughter greeted the "present" and the major used the opportunity to clean the dress of the general's wife, enthusiastically dusting and blowing on it.

"Does not matter! Not worth mentioning" came the friendly protest. "Don't bother, Major Balvan Balvanovich, it is an old dress. Naturally, you understand, to a *bombardirovka* one does not get dressed up like for a ball, although as I see it, when a nice little, well-washed grenade explodes at the right spot, it is more amusing than some long mazurka and firecrackers."

The fourth cannonball tore the pole in two, sending the flag tumbling to the ground.

"Bravo!" roared the soldiers. "A hero! A brave fellow. An officer. This grenade: that one knows its business!"

One of the Finnish guards stepped forward modestly and saluted: "Your Excellency, permit me to return the flag to the roof." "*Durak*," shouted the governor. "Shut up and stand still!"

As if his furlough had been denied, with deep regret, the infantryman slunk back to his place in the line.

However, suddenly, the entire ship became enveloped in dark smoke; only her main mast stuck out from the cloud. There was a hellish crackling, roaring, and thundering at the brick factory, a thick hail of stones, shards, and splinters, and a long, gigantic bang—and from the entire roof and joints, yellow flames were blazing upward. Rage and fury overtook the soldiers and before they could equip and protect themselves, the guards stormed the hill, in disarray, without command or order. They were followed by the major, spouting terrible expletives, going as fast as his noticeable corpulence permitted.

"Back up right away! You dumb beasts! You have nothing to do up there! There is no schnapps there! Or do you think the English sit on their cannonballs like Baron Münchhausen?[26] Then you can wait in vain. They are cowards. They only shoot when they feel safe."

---

[26] Reference to Rudolf Erich Raspe's (1737–1794) story (1785) of a fictional German nobleman who tells about his fabulous adventures, including campaigns against Russia.

"Namely, when they know the enemy had sold the cannonballs," added the governor drily.

In any case, the governor had enough to do, because against his command, irresistibly attracted by the cannons, troops from the palace arrived in a hurry. It took a while, and much abusive language, until order returned, while individual curses of officers still rang out: a precaution to prevent another breakdown of discipline.

The ship fired broadside after broadside in quick succession and, following the wind, a huge cloud of dense smoke danced from one area to another. The horse of the governor's wife turned around on its heels, reared up, and kicked each time a grenade whistled by or smoke reached its nostrils. Balvan Balvanovich, holding the reins tight, and striving to be courtly, tried to joke, claiming that he had observed how eagerly the governor's wife inhaled the smoke and the smell of gun-powder.

"The *Bumbardirovka,* he beamed, "presents you with an *accompanirovanie of perfumirovanie.*"

Pelageya Ivanonvna deigned to find the pun to her liking.

"What's happened to you today, Balvan Balvanovich? Are you ill? You are beginning to worry me. If this continues, there is a danger you will turn out witty in the end. You must cultivate this Balvan Balvanovich, you should!

"I beg you for your kindness, Pelageya Ivanovna; I beg you urgently! Become my doctor! In the whole of

Russia, I could not find a finer and more unblemished one."

"Do me a favor and stop the gallantry! You are as clumsy as a marine officer. Do you really think that I am so stupid as to cure someone else's spirit?"

Balvan Balvanovich's jaw dropped. The general's wife, however, seized with a sudden exuberance for danger—a typical feature of the Russians—suddenly cried out the command: "Let go of the reins!"

As the major obliged, the horse broke into a straight gallop uphill into the middle of the line of fire, toward the burning buildings. A thundering ovation of the soldiers honored her daring, and the major, eagerly limping after her, implored her to return—in vain.

"Let her carry on, the foolish woman!" said the governor, lackadaisically. "If she is that eager to get hit, it is her problem."

And so, Pelageya Ivanovna got her way. Naturally, the horse did not let her stay still on the hilltop. Fearing death, the animal reared up, carried her backward on its hind legs close to the flames until she felt glut scorching her locks and sparks were raining down on the horse's buttocks, upon which, after a few nervous circles, the animal darted down the hill, fleeing unstoppably deep into the town and over the bridge, while the governor's wife, pressing the reins, desperately tried to make it turn left or right, without success.

"How wonderful! Exquisite! What a splendid horse!" she yelled at her husband in a choking voice while passing him in a frenzy.

After a few minutes, she returned from the town, traversing sideways, and forced the anxious, trembling, and steaming animal, now covered in white foam, to trot zigzag back up the rise. When on top, the spinning game began anew, and a few moments later she came hurtling down the hill again.

"But we," asked the captain of the artillery, "Major Balvan Balvanovich, will we not shoot as well?"

"Shoot? Excuse me, with what should we shoot? We have no cannon balls!"

"Just like in the Crimea," murmured the captain gloomily. "God grant Russia the gallows!" Then he talked to his men:

"Patience, brothers. God forbade us using cannon balls."

The soldiers sadly lowered their guns and looked in the air. Meanwhile, something had to be done to greet the *Bombardirovka.*

Therefore, when somewhat later with a hissing sound a stray grenade landed close to the guns, one of the *Gunteroffiziere*,[27] the clown of the garrison, a light-hearted fellow from Kiev, called out:

---

[27] Unteroffiziere (German, non-commissioned officers).

"What do you want here, my little dove? Why are you humming so amorously? I need someone just like you! I have cigarettes, but no matches. Brothers! Today is a holiday! The enemy has presented us with matches!"

With that he rushed toward the grenade. From further away, the officers threw at him the entire rich vocabulary of Russian curses to save him, but all in vain.

"It does not matter. It does not matter at all! Brothers! God is merciful!" he said in a soothing and chivalrous voice, while holding his cigarette casually against the hissing and puffing monstrosity. Then he returned with a satisfied air about him, as if he were drawing on his cigarette. A weak, puffing pop, a tiny red and blue beam of light that flashed in three directions, and the *Gunteroffizier* tossed his head backward, grabbed his backside with his hands, burst in a pitiful scream, and fell to the ground, his body twisting and turning like grapevine.

Cursing, the officers ran to him. Disregarding his pain, a few of his comrades took him by his arms and legs, whatever they could get hold of, and consoled him in their own way.

"Don't scream, you dog!" shouted one. "One could have figured that out! One soldier more or less in the world won't matter. The emperor has enough of them left."

Another one said:

"Now what, brother? So, one dies a little; not much more. What's the big deal? This is the reason for being a soldier!"

Thus they dragged him into town.

The building was burned almost to the ground, but there was no gunfire when a young peasant appeared from Nikolai street in the traditional grey, Finnish shirt, both arms heavy with stones, his face distorted, snorting with rage, from time to time a grim *Satanaperrkele*, leaving his pressed lips. He was followed by a damsel in a blue silk ball-gown, hanging on to him by his shirt, trying to keep up with difficulty, although half dragged by the furious fellow; her train filthy and torn, her hair unraveled into wild strands hanging over her shoulders, her stockings and scarf in loosened disarray.

"Wait, my turtledove! Why are you running like a reindeer?" gasped Agafia, weeping and reproachful. "My God! Stop for a moment!"

However, having seen his destroyed property, Tullela ran even faster, picking up a few stones at random on his way.

"What is he doing? What does he want?" ordered the governor as several bayonets closed off the road in front of the hurrying man.

"Oh, Your Excellency, Baraban Barabanovich" blubbered Agafia, holding tight her fiancé while softly, but determined, she kept throwing down the stones from his arms: "You don't know! This unfortunate, poor thing! It is his house, the enemy has burned down. His house! And we wanted to get married next week! What should we do now? What can we do?"

A murmur of regret ran through the lines, and deeply felt curses were loudly uttered against the Germans, the Turks, and the English because of their inhumane cruelty.

At first somewhat bewildered, the governor regained his composure. Impassioned, he pointed to the smoking building, then at Tullela, denouncing briefly but in a few, powerful words the heinous crime committed by the enemy who were making a mockery of humanity and international law. Thereafter he began working on Tullela.

"Take a look, brothers!" he called out to the soldiers. "Look at this young nondescript Finn, in his simple shirt, without education, without religion, without a job; he could serve as an example for many who boast of their rank and richness. Look at him, at this hero who, without grumbling, happily and voluntarily sacrificed his most precious to the emperor and his fatherland! He beams for joy in the knowledge that by the loss of his property he has saved the town from destruction!"

And stepping up in a military fashion to the unfortunate victim, the governor patted him warmly on the shoulder and continued in a somber voice: "What is your name, you brave man? Don't be ashamed of your name, you have turned it into a name of honor in Russia!"

Tullela, who had let go of the last stones, remained silent for a while, then looking around suspiciously to see whether he was being ridiculed, blurted out his name with a great effort. The general raised his voice in a pathos-filled speech:

"Tullela!" he shouted; "Tullela! Accept the appreciation of your emperor from my lips. Tullela! Holy Russia sends you her thanks and blessings. Tullela, follow this path that you have chosen. Persevere in the future, keep your readiness to sacrifice, so that Finland can be proud to have fathered you, given you birth, have nursed and reared you. Tullela! The place that the enemy has destroyed, you will have again in your heart, larger and more beautiful than it was in real life when it stood in front of you in its awkward and crude shape. Doing the right thing is more virtuous than doing well, and is more precious than profit or possessions. You lost a house and a brick kiln but you have won a cathedral of consciousness; where the hearth used to stand now the altar of the fatherland rests!

"Phew, I am suffocating! How long such speeches are! And tiring! And stupid! Enough! This rascal will be the end of me!"

Upon this, he festively removed one of the twenty-four medals from his chest and pinned the trinket on Tullela's shirt.

"*Urrah!*" shouted the soldiers. The drums rolled.

A somber Tullela stared alternately at his decoration and at the ruins of his house.

"Don't cry, don't be mad, my darling," said Agafia sweetly, holding him lovingly by his arm and opening one of his palms that still clenched a stone. "Now you have a *mandeli*."[28] The gendarmes will greet you when you pass them, and you may stand in the first row at a parade. And during the week before Ash Wednesday, when you lie drunk on the floor, the gendarmes say to one another: 'Do not touch him: he is a brother of the emperor!' And you can lie there undisturbed until next morning. And, you know, when the emperor learns that the enemy had destroyed your house, he will have another one built for you, of marble and gold, with lapis lazuli, like the Isaac Cathedral; he is so rich, one is scared just to think about it! And the emperor will present you with a swing, and a cap with peacock-feathers and a bathroom, with a tall stove one can climb on, and tea with sugar-candy, and a large, yellow Angora cat, and you will be a baron and a high-ranking officer that you can pester anyone whom you dislike and send him to Siberia, straight past Moscow."

"But a man-servant, what do you think Tullela, a man-servant… Would you like to become my man-servant?" asked the general.

---

[28] Mandeli= medals.

Tullela remained silent.

"Of course, he would, naturally" responded Agafia for him. "I mean, until the time the house that the emperor will build us would be ready."

Baraban Barabanovich sneered.

"Silly goose! The emperor has other things to do than to build houses for a cook's sweetheart!"

"How come, Your Excellency? But he will at least give him money to compensate him?"

"I think you are crazy. When it took a hit, it took a hit. What else do we have a war for? Get moving and be soon at home to prepare tea for the mistress because it's getting chilly."

Agafia was baffled, but her carefree nature did not permit any pain to reach her.

"In any case," she consoled him, as she pulled her fiancé along, "do you know my love, from now on you will live with me in the kitchen and sleep at the hearth! I shall make a good fire so that you'll lie in the warmth and in the evening we will play cards and sing the song about the vegetable garden until midnight: 'Agarot, Agarot! Turilili, Turilila.'[29] It will be wonderful, I'm tell-

---

[29] Agar-agar is a vegetarian gelatin substitute produced from a variety of seaweed vegetation. Turilili – turilila is possibly derived from Turai, a vegetable with a strongly ridged green skin and tapered ends which goes by many names, including ridged gourd, silky gourd, and Chinese okra.

ing you, a real pleasure, like a holiday, a walk in the park."

Major Balvan Balvanovich caught up with them; he pushed the Finn out of the way with military roughness and wanted to walk with Agafia, arm in arm. Agafia protected herself with ardor.

"Don't you dare, Balvan Balvanovich, because the governor is jealous and, quite possibly, so is his wife" she added, laughing mischievously.

Balvan Balvanovich sighed. The court martial reappeared in his imagination. Agafia was right, his place in the near future was by the side of the general's wife. Happy for not having been caught, he rushed away from the couple in order to resume his post.

The governor and his wife, too, were on their way home, fighting in marital contentment. "*Durak!*" moaned the general's wife in her magical, melodious and rich voice. "Simply *Durak*. Nothing more, nothing less! How can a man be so stupid as to take the cook's lover into his service?"

"Why? It's really not right to let that poor son-of-a-bitch sleep in the street after his house has been burned to the ground."

"What is right isn't important; but the lover of a cook does not belong in my kitchen. That's all. She will be distracted and ruin the sauces. And if you had just a little bit of common sense, you would have understood that it is also against your own interest that Agafia's darling should be hanging around her all the time."

"Patience, my soul, Patience! Fret not![30] Who says this is how it will remain? This is just the beginning. It shows style: people can see that one has a heart. Tomorrow, there might be a good reason to get rid of the rascal. God is merciful."

While conversing, they reached the entrance of the palace.

Next morning, the man-of-war left its threatening position and pulled back behind the islets of the archipelago, causing happy excitement in the town of Åbo. Even if the danger was not quite over—the *bombardirovka* could begin again in the evening—it seemed that such a signal from the enemy displayed a considered regularity which protected the inhabitants from unpleasant surprises, and the silent promise to safeguard the population had been kept as well. Why would they have sent off the warning rockets, before the cannonballs began to fly? That was not the wild, barbaric desire to kill and scorch and the lack of all humanity, as they had been depicted. To anchor at a spot from where they could have burned down the entire town, only to satisfy themselves with a lone brick kiln: that displayed planning and benevolent planning to boot. Did the enemy merely wanted to show its power symbolically, or was

---

[30] Fret not! is quoting Psalm 37:7.

this one of the original, typically English acts of folly? There were many lively discussions about this subject, but no longer in a bitter mood, but rather with satisfaction, even respect. Curiosity how the *bombardirovka* would conclude, got intermixed with a certain joy over the uncertainty bringing a welcome change to that remote and boring coastal nest.

Meanwhile, the governor had loud scenes with his wife about getting the useless Tullela out of the house that turned out to be not very difficult, because the governor had been right: God was merciful! Also, in order to achieve her purpose, Pelageya Ivanovna used her talents to utter such plaintive sounds that one could think it was she, and not Tullela, facing expulsion. At the same time, Agafia wept buckets like the cats at the grave of *Struwwelpeter*.[31] She would have wanted to follow her fiancé had it not been her wages, still held back by the mistress. That sum, by then, accounted for the entire fortune of the two lovers. Although temporarily downcast, her loveliness, youth and good health, her childish trust in God, and her habit to console others, cut short Agafia's sadness. Still sobbing about their losses, as she walked Tullela down the steps, they barely reached the street when Agafia smiled at him cheerfully and ordered

---

[31] Heinrich Hoffmann's (1809–1894) *Struwwelpeter* was first published in German in 1844. It appeared in English translation as *Struwwelpeter. Merry Tales and Funny Pictures* in 1848.

him to return for a secret visit that very night, promising that she would save something good for him to eat, and would keep the samovar warm. And then, with her fine little paws, she pushed a handful of sugar quickly in his mouth.

"Now kiss me my turtledove!" she demanded. "One more time! More!"

She performed for him her most solemn bow, then giggling and laughing, she skipped flirtatiously up the stairs.

Tullela remained standing there, at a loss, looking up and down the street. A window flew open above him.

"Hell!" roared the governor's voice and, right away, the window closed with a clink.

Tullela wobbled slowly to the pastor.

"Pappi," he began meekly, twirling his cap in his hands, "give me a job."

The pastor who knew about the misfortune that hit the innocent man, felt sorry for him.

"What kind of a job would you like?"

"I don't know."

"What can you do, and what do you know?"

"Nothing."

"But you know how to read and write?'

"I do."

"And probably you also understand Swedish?"

"I do."

"And German?"

"A little."

"And Russian?"

"A little."

"And what else?"

"Nothing."

"Nothing at all?"

"That one learned in school."

The pastor tried to ask a few more questions, and then gave him a friendly pat on his shoulder.

"You are a good lad, Tullela! You have learned diligently, just as a real Finn should. Hold you head high like Gustav Vasa in front of the *riksdag* of Västerås,[32] and sing for me hymn number sixteen from the *Book of Psalms*. I hope you know the *Book of Psalms* by heart?"

"Yes, I do," said Tullela uneasily.

Then he stood upright, arms hanging clumsily, looked stiffly at the pastor and began singing in a booming voice that made the walls tremble.

"Fine!" declared the pastor after several stanzas. "Would you like to be a cantor in my parish?"

"Yes, I would."

"Then let's ask the Almighty for His blessing. We are having a service this morning to give thanks for the lib-

---

[32] Gustav Vasa (Gustav I), King of Sweden (1496–1560) called together the *riksdag* (parliament) in Västerås. There, the decision was made to convert Sweden into a Protestant state. The king's statue, completed in 1864, stands in Västerås.

eration of our town from the hands of our enemies, and we are going to sing the sixteenth psalm."

Half an hour later, Tullela walked to the church behind his Pappi, in the black gown of the choir.

Pelageya Ivanovna, happy to have succeeded in keeping Agafia in her service, and pleasantly tired after the exertions of a night spent awake on horseback—which put her in a better mood than eating or sleeping—paid a visit to her husband's study in order to sermonize a little for the sake of practice.

"Pray, tell me, what should this mean? Is this how we have to live? Now, that everything went better than we had hoped, you could spare a few moments also for your wife!"

"That will not work, my little dove, will not work at all. It is a nightmare how much I have to do."

"Nonsense! You can tell this to someone else. A governor never has anything to do."

"But for heaven's sake, think about it, my love, I must send a report about the *bombardirovka* to Petersburg. I can hardly imagine that *you* have anything against getting compensated for the losses we have suffered. Right? I hope it will also initiate a reward and a promotion. In any case, it does not harm to try."

"You could have told me this right away, my friend! That is something quite different. Of course, by all means, you must request compensation! And for goodness' sake, don't be so modest again like last time; this is your greatest shortcoming. Who will thank you? Not a soul! You know how they are in Petersburg. Unless a civil servant continuously demands money, till they don't know where their head is at, they think he's not making any effort. Just hammer on them! And add a neat little zero to it! Round it out! Don't be bashful! For what else is the state there? The kiln alone is worth about twice a hundred thousand rubles, plus the depletion of weapons and ammunition, compensating the victims, wage increases for the officers and the sergeants who had served with distinction, the digging of trenches we had to prepare to avoid a possible further attack, and the anxiety I had suffered for which for years I will have to be treated in spas, and so on and so forth. We cannot get along forever without horses either. One has to honor the office; this is as important for the emperor as for us."

"But horses, my dearest Pelageya Ivanovna, horses cost a lot of money. That means, one must have a coachman and oats and hay. And the stable is in disorder. That too must be repaired."

"Have mercy! Baraban Barabanovich, you are no longer a child! Who says we have to keep the horses? That's all we would need! For whom? For the few Swedish women who run around like cooks? Or for the Lutheran pastors? No, thank you. The only bearable thing in this godforsaken German hole is that one can at least save some money. Balvan Balvanovich will buy the horses from you. He needs them desperately. Just last week he wrote about them to Petersburg. Speaking of Balvan Balvanovich, do you know, my love, that deep down he is all heart, even if a touch rough and uneducated. Surely you wouldn't be so stupid as to report him for those few puny irregularities?"

"Don't fret, my darling, I wouldn't think of it. Why should anything like that be the business of the folks in Petersburg? I will just give him a dressing down. Voilà tout!"

Having completed his report and sent it off with his adjutant, he rubbed his hands.

"Stupid fellows, these English," he said to himself scornfully. "They have bombarded us with rubles. Would you, gentlemen, perhaps care to do it over? I am at your service! Please! You would do me a favor!"

Thereafter, he strutted cheerfully over to the major's living quarters, reprimanding the latter, who was awake but still enveloped in the eiderdown of his bed, and told him off in a suppressed voice, until the man became as soft as kid-gloves, and swore upon all the saints that he would never again steal only for his own enrichment.

"But cigars, Your Excellency," the major finished the affirmation of his promises. "May I offer you some cigars?"

The governor was stunned.

"Cigars? How so? From where come those cigars?"

Grinning, the major explained: "They are authentic, from Tenkado, the tobacconist on Nevsky-Prospect.[33] I received them yesterday by courier. A light? Baraban Barabanovich? May I? Here! May I have the honor! And I have ordered for Pelageya Ivanovna two thousand cigarettes, genuine *La Ferme*, the strong ones; this afternoon, if you permit me the pleasure, I shall deliver them in person."

"What a charming cavalier you are, basically, Balvan Balvanovich! Always attentive, always gallant. My wife has been longing for cigarettes for ages. Imagine, just imagine, she has no more than eighty left. And with the war, how can one get hold of more in a hurry? Say what you want, but it is a rather unpleasant thing, such a war. I have the honor, Balvan Balvanovich."

As the governor returned to his palace, a large number of people were waiting for him in front.

"What's going on?" he asked a soldier.

"An English truce negotiator, Your Excellency."

"How come? Will the entire thing start all over again?"

"Precisely, Your Excellency, as you say. It begins anew. Namely, if you so order it, Your Excellency!"

---

[33] Nevsky Prospekt is St. Petersburg's main avenue and one of its most famous streets, cutting through the historical center of the city.

The governor entered his palace laughing, and called out to the peace negotiator from still far away:

"A second *bombardirovka?* I am at your service."

After a brief greeting, the Englishman responded stiffly and phlegmatically:

"No, Your Excellency, we are moving on today; I came to add up the costs and compensate for the damage."

At first Baraban Barabanovich thought he had misheard the man. But since he had open ears and a sharp mind when it came to payments coming from others, a true genius, he immediately transposed himself into the new situation, and began to hike up the sum.

"Gentlemen, that pleasure will cost you six-hundred thousand rubles; not one kopek less. And this can still be considered a present. A brand new, excellent brick factory, completed merely six months ago, with lodgings, barn and garden, and brand new furniture. A real jewel case, I am telling you. Six hundred thousand in cash or we blow up your ship. You must admit, you have been caught in a mouse-trap. In the archipelago we have masked guns surrounding you and the entire seafloor is mined."

The Englishman insisted on checking out the damage on his own. He was blindfolded and led to the burned out area, all the while constantly harassed with persuasive talk, and with each step the amount of compensation grew.

Having inspected the piles of rubble, the truce nego-tiator declared calmly: "Four-hundred thousand rubles."

A stunned murmur, even bewilderment, greeted this sum that was at least six times more than the actual loss had been. Only the governor gestured desperately when he called upon the saints of both sides of the Ural Mountain to bear witness to how miserably he had been cheated. Finally, when the truce envoy was ready to leave, did he sigh:

"Sir, you count on the kind-heartedness of the Rus-sians. It is well-known that the Russian is like a child to whom they can offer anything they feel like. Well, you are right; we will never get totally rid of this flaw, although we have been frequently taken advantage of because of it. Well, in the name of God, if there is no other way, hand me over the sum, for the sake of peace."

"Where is the proprietor?" asked the Englishman.

The governor turned deathly pale.

"What about the proprietor?" he asked, grinding his teeth. "Unless you think I want to embezzle the money?"

The truce negotiator insisted on his wish and stood calmly, like a sentinel, until Tullela was found in the church and was brought there, still dressed in his sur-plice.

At that point, the Englishman requested the mayor to serve as a witness but when he showed up, he had to return home because he forgot to put on his official sash. Then he hung the sash over his left shoulder, instead of the right. The tension kept growing and the people became irritated, assuming that the delay was just an excuse to refuse paying in the end. However, the negotiator uttered his "Everything is in order," and without further ado, opened his large briefcase, filled with banknotes.

"I believe you're crazy!" snorted the governor: "You are not going to pay four-hundred thousand rubles to this scoundrel for his wretched, pathetic, and musty hut! The fellow is robbing you in the most outrageous manner! Not forty thousand, not twenty thousand, not even ten thousand is it worth. Give the rascal a tip, a kick in the ass, and godspeed!

The Englishman could not care less about the general's fury. He paid the sum into Tullela's hands and made the town's mayor sign a receipt. Thereafter he declared his mission accomplished, called for his blindfold, and left for the port, led by a soldier and followed by a gigantic, ever growing, respectful crowd, with cap in hand.

The same afternoon when the frigate, ready to leave for Björneborg,[34] began lifting anchor, half a dozen fishing boats sporting white flags swayed among the islets. They were let through, one by one, in order to respect

---

[34] Björneborg (Swedish) = Pori, town in Finland.

the safety code and out of fussiness. They were simple Finnish peasants, unarmed, embarrassed, rolling their caps in their hands, not knowing what to say. Finally their leader began:

"Erre Majori,[35] we live on the second islet, up there, opposite to the mouth of the river. Life is very hard during times like this, Erre Leutenanti! We cannot sell anything in Tukholmi[36] because of the war, and there is no money in Finland. Erre Kapitäni, since we are Lutherans, Erre Generali, a little—you know, Pummi, Tulipummi, Pumpartirovaniri our village, Erre Atmirali, if you would be so kind, we beg you."

The request of the other deputations sounded similar. And that's how it went on all the way to Björneborg. but, outside the archipelago, an entire flotilla lay in waiting. They forced the English—outraged over the fishermen's immense desire to be bombed—to turn fast toward the south, hoping that in Helsinki they would meet a somewhat more accessible, genuinely hostile population.

It must have been about three weeks after the departure of the English, when against all begging and admonition, Agafia left her service, in order to get married, relinquishing her wages, which were later sent to her as an act of grace, when one morning ominous things happened in the governor's study. Baraban Barabanovich

---

[35] Erre is the local Finnish version for the German *Herr*.
[36] Finnish name of Stockholm (Sweden).

and Balvan Balvanovich sat silently in the middle of the room, pale as two miserable sinners, permanently wheezing for air and excuses. A distinguished looking young man, wearing an elegant civilian suit, sat at the desk, drawing on a cigarette. Periodically gesturing lazily with his hand and looking half way over his shoulder, he directed a question in a thin but sharp tone to one of the men, or perhaps to both at the same time.

"Gentlemen, on June 2, at your request, we sent you three thousand guns. You might not find it troublesome to advise me what has happened to those weapons?"

The general and the major coughed nervously, looking for a possible explanation.

"Fine. I understand. I thank you. There is no need to exert yourselves further. But unless it takes too much effort, perhaps you would be so kind to advise me why the work on the entrenchment for the defense of the coast, for which you have collected money and material for the past two years, has not begun?"

"What do you mean it has not begun?" exhaled Balvan Balvanovich in an artificial fury. "You can see the ditches right at the castle, Feodor Grigorovich! You can see them with your own eyes, Feodor Grigorovich! Please take the trouble and I shall show them to you, myself!"

With that he rose from his chair.

"Quite unnecessary, Balvan Balvanovich! I would not inconvenience you with that. Please return to your seat. Not for a minute do I doubt what you claim. The trenches are at the castle, you say so, and therefore I believe it. I believe it especially, because they have been there for the past twenty six years and have been paid for by us five times so far, as I can prove this fact from the documents, if you bother to look at them for confirmation."

It went on in this manner for long, unending hours, taking up the entire morning. The unfortunate officers looked longingly at the door for a savior, but all in vain. The terrifying young gentleman had turned the key from the inside. Finally, at half past one, Feodor Grigorovich lit a fresh cigarette, closed his dossier carefully, stood up, bowed and declared with an engaging smile:

"Gentlemen, this is fine. I thank you; we are through! Please forgive me for being forced to take so much of your time. Permit me, if now, at the end, to ask if it were perhaps possible for you to accompany me to Petersburg, right after breakfast? It is more comfortable there and one can work much better in the Ministry of War."

Upon the news, the two wrongdoers who just rose, almost keeled over and had to hold on to their chairs. Now, facing the unavoidable punishment, they lost even their dignity.

"I beg you, Feodor Grigorovich" pleaded Balvan Balvanovich, pressing himself on the investigating civil servant, "what do you benefit from it if we are demoted and deported? You, too, are serving the state. What would happen to our poor fatherland if we kept denouncing one another?"

Without moving a muscle in his face, the civil servant shrugged regretfully.

"Sir, permit me to tell you," said Baraban Barabanovich, with a touch of tenderness mixed into his proud military voice, "you are, as I conclude from your elegant use of the language and clothing, also familiar with Paris and therefore know the dictates of gallantry. I have a wife, Feodor Grigorovich: the agony over my shame would kill her."

Feodor Grigorovich bowed.

"My position is painful when it forces me to cause concerns to a lady, however I am commanded by my duty and my conscience."

Suddenly the major regained his ill temper.

"Duty and conscience?" he thundered, "duty and conscience? Have mercy! And you want to be a Russian, Feodor Grigorovich? Do me a favor and leave the double-talk to the Germans and the English.

Feodor Grigorovich turned pale; his lips trembled. Casting a penetrating, murderous glance that cut into the major, he said haughtily:

71

"Possibly, Balvan Balvanovich, even probably, there is still some sense of duty and conscience present among the Russians. Not all of them are thieves and scoundrels, although our state crawls with them as salamanders in the swamp. But as far as I am concerned, give me the benefit of the doubt that I am going to aid my people to clean up the swamp. You can leave it to me, Balvan Balvanovich, even if I have to send regiments of generals, colonels, and majors to Siberia."

"Don't be angry, Feodor Grigorovich, because of an ill-considered word," said the governor trying to mollify him.

But by then the man stood at the door and, giving the officers a brief, contemptuous look, turned the key with trembling hands. But when he opened the door, he stood startled and motionless, while his pale, nervously twitching cheeks turned a deep red.

Dressed in black silk, the governor's wife stood in front of the door: beautiful, like an angel, tempting like a Polish woman and noble like a Russian lady. A soft smile spread over her entire being as she greeted the angry guest, and since she immediately saw the effect her beauty had on him, she found the most natural modulation of voice in her register:

"How happy I am to have the honor, finally! You know, gentlemen, I have been standing here at the door waiting like an odalisque for the sultan, to have the pleasure of inviting all of you to share our breakfast. You are not gallant, you must admit, not to have felt my proximity in your hearts. One notices this after marriage and as one is growing old. Sir, I have to thank you, since you must have entertained my husband splendidly, because he entirely forgot about his breakfast; this has not happened to him for a whole year. May I ask for your arm to lead me to the dining room? To tell youth the truth, I am trembling for fear of what you will think of me; I am afraid to confess that since Agafia has become unfaithful to me, I have a silly Finnish goose as our cook, therefore, will you forgive me, I cannot offer for breakfast more than salmon, a roast, and a creme of game. Balvan Balvanovich, with you I do not have to be formal! You are, after all, an old and beloved friend of our house. You must eat with us in honor of our special guest!"

Feodor Grigorovich, hit in the heart by the magic of the temptress, defended himself in a like manner:

"Madame, as hard as it is for me to refuse the pleasure," he responded stuttering, "I cannot accept your kind invitation. I am not alone: Two officers with whom I have arrived here from Petersburg are waiting for me at the inn."

"What a pity!" she lamented. "But, permit me, what is your name?"

"Feodor Grigorovich."

"What a pity, Feodor Grigorovich! Naturally, I would not presume to influence your decision. Even less so would I insist, since you would have to do without the company of my husband during breakfast. He has urgent business at the palace, where he has to stay until late evening. And Balvan Balvanovich never lets himself be invited, no matter how one begs him. The company of a lone lady, from the provinces to boot, offers too little excitement for a young gentleman from Petersburg to expect that it would suffice."

Feodor Grigorovich still stood there bravely, although silent and deathly pale, his lips trembling. Meanwhile the general made good use of the man's hesitation.

"Then tonight," he spoke freely and naturally, with the gallantry of the lord of the house. "May I hope that you will excuse my absence until then?"

And before he could be corrected, he disappeared.

A vague notion about his chances to be saved took shape even behind Balvan Balavanovich's low forehead, but the idea of salmon and game fought hard in his innermost thoughts, thus it took several unambiguous glances from the governor's wife until he decided to withdraw.

"The pleasure was mine" he rumbled finally at his leave-taking, but wanting to demonstrate that he was anything but stupid, he winked and added play-fully, "I wish you a merry breakfast, Feodor Grig-orovich!"

The young man jumped up, as if bitten by a scor-pion, but he was immediately softened by the forth-coming style of Pelageya Ivanonvna.

"Do not be angry, Feodor Grigorovich!" she im-plored him, and placed her hand on his arm. "He is an uneducated, rough soldier. And if anyone should be offended by his lack of manners, truly, it should be me. And now, you would not want me to pay for his tact-lessness? How would a poor, lonely woman be respon-sible for that? Come, Feodor Grigorovich, I am as happy as a child to hear from you about Petersburg and the Court. I am sure you are at home in that world.

Feodor Grigorovich tried to remove his arm and held back his step. But all of a sudden, without know-ing how and why, he kissed the woman's hand violently. With an easy smile the governor's wife let him know of her appreciation.

"You see, here we have the true, gallant man of the world. You know what good manners are, Feodor Grigorovich, I believe, we shall understand each other! My God! Here in these miserable haunts, one is not spoiled by chivalry. No, you are the first to know. Please, this is my home. Well if you absolutely insist..."

Soon thereafter, Baraban Barabanovich Stupenkin was awarded the Alexander-Nevsky-Order[37] for his heroic defense of the town of Åbo, with an annual honorary pension of ten thousand rubles irrespective of his military promotion, and a transfer to one of the most sumptuous districts of southern Russia, where Pelageya Ivanovna had the opportunity to hire three cooks instead of one to have her game prepared in a Swedish sauce. Balvan Balvanovich, in consideration of his outstanding conduct during the bombardment, was promoted to colonel.

In the beginning of the following year, Tullela built a large schnapps distillery, large enough to still the thirst of the whole of Finland, near Vyborg, because Agafia wanted to live close to the Russian border so in the winter she could travel in their coach to the 'Swiss mountains'[38] of Petersburg. In the fall, when the charitable institution was completed, they held a splendid wedding at the *Societäthüss,* where an immense amount of almonds, hazelnuts, nougats, baba, and sugar-candy was distributed. Balvan Balvanovich and the mayor

---

[37] Alexander Nevsky (1221–1263) was prince of Novgorod and then grand prince of Vladimir. A legendary military leader and states- man, he defeated the Swedes at the Neva River.

[38] "Swiss mountains," a nickname given to the Duderhof Hills outside of St. Petersburg on account of their height over the surrounding landscape and their popularity as a winter vacation destination.

were best men, the orchestra played the music of the regiment, and after the meal a number of Cossacks appeared from the garrison, dancing in the streets, making noise, and drinking until they lay in heaps on the ground, like in Paradise.

"What have I told you, Tullela?" asked a delighted Agafia with an impish smile when, during the evening, with the shimmering wedding-crown on her head, she climbed over the mounds of unconscious men to reach their carriage in the street. "God is merciful! Yesterday *bombardirovka*, today wedding with almonds! This shows that he is a God of the right kind, a Russian, a good one. Do you hear me? You know, my turtledove, now you are an important, rich gentleman, no one's subject but the emperor's. From now on, when I say: "Do you hear me?" You must always answer: "At your service," just like an educated gentleman.

"At your service," murmured Tullela.

Thereafter, they climbed into their hansom and galloped to Tammerfors[39] for their honeymoon.

"How amusing, how wonderful" rejoiced Agafia, her bones banging, as she was thrown around in the hard carriage like chaff on the threshing-floor; on the tick like in a telega.

Out of gratitude, the pastor in Åbo, who in Tullela's greatest need appointed him cantor, was made the

---

[39] Tampere in Finnish. A town in western Finland.

schnapps-inspector of the Vyborg district, where Tullela soon gained great influence in the local administration.

Yet, to this very day, when hearing of a person who has become suddenly rich and is showing off with his wealth, the Swedes of Åbo say, "the lucky fellow! Just look at him! My goodness! He either inherited from his uncle, the Devil of Vexjö,[40] or he had been bombarded by the English!"

---

[40] A town in southern Sweden.

BIOGRAPHICAL NOTE

on Carl Spitteler[1]

I was born on April 24, 1845, in the little town of Liestal in the Canton of Baselland. When I was four we moved to Bern, where my father had been appointed treasurer of the newly established Swiss Confederacy. In the winter of 1856–57 I returned home with my parents. I attended the Gymnasium at Basle and lived with an aunt; later I lived in Liestal and went by train to Basle daily to attend the Obergymnasium called the "Pädagogium." Wilhelm Wackernagel and Jacob Burckhardt were my teachers there. At my father's request I took up the study of law at the University of Zürich in 1863. Later, 1865–70, I studied theology in Zürich, Heidelberg, and Basle. After taking my theological examination at Basle I

[1] Carl Spitteler wrote this autobiography at the time of the Nobel award, in 1919, and it was first published in the book series *Les Prix Nobel.* It was later edited and republished in *Nobel Lectures, Literature 1901–1967*, edited by Horst Frenz (Elsevier Publishing Company, Amsterdam, 1969). Available online: https://www. nobelprize.org/prizes/literature/1919/spitteler/biographical/.

went to Petersburg at the invitation of General Standertskjöld to be the tutor of his younger children. I left for Petersburg in August, 1871 and stayed there until 1879. During this period, spent partly in Russia and partly in Finland, I worked on *Prometheus und Epimetheus*, which, after my return to Switzerland, I published in 1881 at my own expense under the pseudonym Carl Felix Tandem. The book was completely neglected; because it was not even reviewed I abandoned all hope of making poetry my living and was compelled instead to teach school (Neuveville, Canton Bern, 1881–1885) and work for newspapers (*Grenzpost*, Basle, 1885–86; *Neue Zürcher Zeitung*, 1890–92). In July, 1892, fate suddenly granted me financial independence. I moved to Lucerne, where I have lived happily with my family ever since. The following works of mine appeared after *Prometheus und Epimetheus: Extramundana* (1883), a book which I consider mediocre; *Schmetterlinge* (1889) [Butterflies]; *Friedli der Kolderi* (1891); *Gustav* (1892); *Litterarische Gleichnisse* (1892) [Literary Parables]; *Balladen* (1896); *Der Gotthard* (897); *Conrad der Leutnant* (1898); *Lachende Wahrheiten* (1898) *Laughing Truths*]. Between 1900 and 1906 the four volumes of my epic *Olympischer Frühling* [Olympian Spring] were published: I. *Die Auffahrt* [Overture]; II. *Hera die Braut* [Hera the Bride]; III. *Die Hohe Zeit* [High Tide]; IV. *Ende und Wende* [End and Change]. [...]

In 1909 a revised edition of my epic in five volumes was published; by the end of 1920 it had run into several editions. After *Olympischer Frühling* I published *Glockenlieder* (1906) [Bell Songs]; *Imago* (1908); *Gerold und Hansli, die Mädchenfeinde* (1907) [*Two Little Misogynists*], translated into several languages; and *Meine frühesten Erlebnisse* (1914) [My Earliest Experiences].

Carl Spitteler in 1905

ABOUT THE TRANSLATOR

Marianna D. Birnbaum is Research Professor at the University of California at Los Angeles where she has been teaching for several decades. She also served as recurring visiting faculty or Chair of MA Examination Committees of the Central European University since its foundation.

Author of over twenty monographs and more than a hundred articles and chapters in scholarly publications, Birnbaum's research focuses on Central European culture from the Renaissance to date.